ONE IS ONE

ONE IS ONE

JOHN RANKINE

LONDON : DENNIS DOBSON

First published in Great Britain in 1968 by
Dobson Books Ltd, 80 Kensington Church Street, London, W.8

Printed by Clarke, Doble and Brendon Ltd
Cattedown, Plymouth
SBN 234 77065 1

CHAPTER ONE

SENIOR Controller Dag Fletcher stubbed the repeat button, with a quick decisive jab, and settled back in his swivel chair to hear it all again. In the seconds it took to sort itself out, he turned away from his admin console and watched an incoming ship on to its pad. From this high window in the European Space Corporation H.Q. block, he had a panoramic view of the complex; an ant hill of some ten thousand personnel to keep the silver ships moving about the galaxy.

Against his knowledge of every aspect of space fleet operation, he had to evaluate the spiel from the psychological assessment lab. It was all meretricious stuff; but for his money it told only a tiny fraction of the human story. Psychometrics had its place. Centuries of experience underpinned its main theoretical predictions. Group wise, it was very good and could tell you a good deal about how an average man would behave. Its weakness lay in the fact that there was no average man, living or dead. The only acid test of any individual was what he made of a whole life and no test could simulate that. There was a valid point there, of course, you couldn't wait that long to find out.

By this time, the cool, precise voice of the records librarian was in full spate and he listened again to the breakdown of test results on Vernon Spencer. He spared a thought to wonder whether Paul V. Spencer, the Corporation's Chairman, had yet had this report on his nephew. Probably not, or he would have been down from his penthouse, gunning for somebody. It was certainly a stinker and hearing it twice produced no new, favourable nuance on any part of it. Stress tolerance below any acceptable level, suggestibility high, a cluster of attitude ratings which would have looked at home on a profile card for a criminal lunatic.

Fletcher had heard enough and from his memory of the young crewman did not believe a word of it. Even the accompanying picture record which was simultaneously screened for him was incongruous. Thin featured, dark, wiry build, the young Spencer had an 'attack' at some of the traditional survival and command problems which belied the figures in the report. It was at this point in training that all the information came together. Either it went forward with his O.K. for the next stage or the man was out. It was a part of the job that he did not much like. The axeman. Playing God. Five years intensive work and a word from him made it pointless. But it was a function he would not delegate.

This time there was the extra complication of Spencer's uncle. But he put it squarely to himself that it would be just as wrong to refuse to give the man a break for fear of being accused of favouritism, as it would be to accept him for any reason at all other than proven suitability. That reasoning was getting complex, so he stopped thinking and acted as he always did, when it came to the crunch, on instinct.

He dictated, 'Six months extension and review. Place this man on the next training flight. Let me see all relevant reports again at the end of that time. Period.'

Two hours later, on the afternoon conference with departmental heads and Chairman Spencer bringing up a request for a replanning of perimeter routes, he had occasion to remember it. It now seemed likely that the first commander to have the privilege of Vernon Spencer's services would be himself. If his hunch was a bad one, he would be the one to regret it.

Paul V. Spencer had been droning on for some time in his unctuous, umbilical way, when Dag came out of a reverie, brought on by the striking elegance of the chief executive of the women's training wing. What traumatic experience had winkled her out of her customary uniform could hardly be guessed at; but she now sat literally revealed in a negligible frivolity of pale grey lace. He was shifting circumspectly round to see how this confection was carried on below table level, when the actual words Spencer was using began to make sense in his head.

'And so we can kill two birds with one stone—to coin a phrase, and use this schedule-setting mission as a final training run for some of our senior students. With a crew of eleven, and using *Interstellar X*, we can afford to have five or six trainees. It will be a straightforward run on established routes with no special navigational problems.'

That sounded to Fletcher like a famous last word. He had never yet taken a ship out when there were not special problems. That was what the long training was all about. It was not a land based transport system with a depot round every corner. *Interstellar X* too. He had privately decided that no one but himself would take that ship up for some years yet.

Interstellar X was an obsolescent I.G.O. military corvette. The Inter Galactic Organisation had put it at the Corporation's disposal for special missions. It had largely been at Fletcher's request and because of his old associations with I.G.O. top brass, that the Corporation had been allowed to retain it with all its protective equipment intact.

He found himself speaking into the silence that flowed in when Spencer's rumblings died out. 'Yes. I believe it will be best to use *Interstellar X*. It costs more in fuel of course; but we save in every other way. No regular ship taken off another route. No dislocation of existing crews. A quicker round trip. It will be ideal from the navigational angle, because an error, which might be fatal on a freighter, could be corrected, down to the last second before impact, with the power available there. I'm very interested in this last bunch of crewmen. I'll take it up myself. If that is agreeable to this conference.'

It was two days before he could send in a crew list how-ever. When it finally showed up on Spencer's flight board, it had eleven names.

Commander:	D. Fletcher
Co-Pilot:	Capt. Bradley Heald
Navigation:	1. Lieut. Bruce Charlton
	2. Freya Burleigh
	3. Vernon Spencer
Power:	1. Lieut. Stuart Marsh
	2. Jacqueline Ann Roth
	3. Don Voller
Communications:	1. Lieut. Tamar Kelly
	2. Richard Campbell
	3. Les Rooney.

That put in six trainees; numbers two and three in each section. Four men and two women. The three executives in the number one slot were top level. Heald was very senior, a man of long experience, only missing independent command by a fraction. Too late now, age-wise. This would probably be his last mission.

Fletcher was running over the programme for the next quarter with the man he would leave in charge of it, when the Summons came from above. The video glowed brilliant purple as his secretary, Vanessa, filled it with her latest coiffure. Giving him two seconds to get the full treatment, she lifted her head to say, 'The Chairman is asking you if you could spare him a little time as of now.'

'Tell him I'll be there in two minutes.'

Fletcher turned back to his second in command, 'I'll go and see Spencer; all clear from your point of view?'

'Crystal. It looks like a trouble free run.'

'It always does and never is; but I'm sure you'll handle it. If you can get Vanessa settled in a permanent hair style you'll have done well.'

Fletcher went behind his admin console and signalled for

his private elevator. A section of plain wall ran back and showed a bronze grille, which itself began a silent, portcullis movement into the ceiling. Then he was going up to the penthouse.

He found Spencer seated facing the door and had begun to speak to him before he realised that the Chairman was not alone. A dapper figure in the black and silver uniform of high ranking I.G.O. executives came out of the depths of a chair which had its back to the door and Spencer was interrupting him to say, 'Someone you know, I think, Dag. And a proposition that might make you want to revise this crew list.'

The I.G.O. man was coming forward with both hands outstretched.

'Good to see you again, Commander. As you will guess, I'm here to beg a favour. But nothing out of the way this time.'

Dag recognised the commissar Kandmark with an equal pleasure. 'It's been a long time, but you're looking as fit as always. What is it this time then?'

Spencer joined the reunion with, 'It's the checking run, Dag. As soon as the flight details were sent in to I.G.O. they alerted the commissar to ask for an inspection team to be included.'

That was normal I.G.O. practice. The central organisation relied on planetary fleets to feed in information and to assist in the routine chores of investigation on new routes. Their own fleets of military craft were maintained almost exclusively for patrol and peace keeping activities.

'What's the reference?'

Kandmark said, 'Thirza. It's on a solar system on the edge of our space. Not visited so far; but it's come up for detailed investigation on the normal list. Probes show interesting features. Atmosphere is O.K. Mineral deposits by spectrum analysis appear to be exceptionally rich. Platinum particularly. Naturally this is top secret. It's near enough to Outer

Galactic Alliance territory to make them put in a claim if it
was thought to be worth while.'

'What exactly do you want me to do?'

'Take in Thirza on your route. Do a sample survey. Set
up a token I.G.O. consulate. That will make ownership clear.
Drop ore samples at Fingalna on the way back. We will see
to them from there. Nothing to it.'

'That I have heard before.'

'Truly, Dag. It's straightforward.'

'I could not afford to leave personnel behind on Thirza.'

'No, and it won't be necessary. There is an I.G.O. commissar to be picked up on the way. He will stay there. And
two geological experts to do the survey. Really you haven't
a thing to worry about.'

'It sounds all right. There's room of course in *Interstellar
X* for three extra. Who are they?'

'Commissar Cormac, Dr. Tancred and his assistant. They
will probably stay behind also. I.G.O. will send out a full
diplomatic team to take over. But you don't have to wait for
that.'

'Well, I can't really object. I don't see that we need to alter
anything in our arrangements. As you say, it's a simple
matter. Do you agree, Chairman?'

'Yes, I'm sure the committee will be glad to help in any
way they can and this really does not put out any time
schedules at all.'

It was a point. They were building credit on the I.G.O.
account at very little expense.

Spencer got back to the original point. 'What about the
crew Dag? Will this extension of the mission make enough
difference to warrant a revision?'

Fletcher was a good half minute weighing it up. When he
finally spoke, he had accepted a number of risks in a field
where he had always claimed to make certain, first, last and
all the time. Who was it had said that risk taking enhanced
sensitivity? More than likely it accelerated the complete

insensitivity of *rigor mortis*. However, he sounded absolutely convincing when he said, 'Not at all, there's some good material there. I'll stick with that. I could not have spared anyone for the stake-claiming chore, but that aside we'll be all right.'

Kandmark said, 'Then my purpose is successful. I need hardly say that the whole matter is top secret. Thirza, as I said, is not far from Outer Galactic Alliance space. If they were to get wind of this, they would try to get in first with a claim and possible occupation. They would have no right of course, but a long period of litigation would follow and possession would be nine points of the law. Thirza is the code name on the security file. I will leave the detailed stellar fix under seal. It will be for opening only after Fingalna. Even the specialists you are to pick up there do not know the location. You will be confirmed in I.G.O. rank for the mission. We could not have a better man for the job. Thank you both.'

When he had gone, Spencer said, 'Now that you have agreed the crew list, I must add my personal thanks. I don't know what young Vernon is up to; but you would have had every good reason to put him out. I couldn't have wished for a better introduction to the service than a trip under your command.'

It was a far cry from the days when Spencer and his Senior Controller had been at cross purposes over every issue in the book. Dag said, 'A very handsome compliment, Chairman. Be sure that I'll take a close look at him. If there's any truth in those reports that is exactly what will happen when we get back.'

'I shall quite understand that.'

Vernon Spencer himself was not as conscious of his good fortune. When the list went up on the training wing board, he did not clap his tiny hands with glee. For the record, he said to Jacqueline Ann Roth who had gone, hand in hand, down the corridor with him to take a look. 'Well, the old bastard. He's fixed that. Fletcher too. They want to see me wreck a real ship before they take the hint.'

'What's wrong with you V? You can do the mathematics of it with half your head. Why not do the graceful thing? Qualify to please your Uncle. Spend a year or two at it, then retire into whatever it is you've set your mind on.'

Jacqueline Ann gave him the benefit of a straight, rather impatient stare from wide apart, grey flecked eyes. She was vividly dark, slightly built, hair black and straight like a lacquered skull cap. Tight pink sweater pulled into a heavy gold belt and white pants. Her voice was precise and clipped. Speaking in the dark, she would be listed as 'managing witch grade one'. But in the light of midday, she got indulgent attention.

'A year or two you say. Spend a year or two moving my body round the galaxy in one of these God-forsaken tin tubes. I can't think of anything worse. I'll take this trip though. By God, I'll show him this time. He won't want me on one of his ships again.'

'Watch it. Remember the rest of the crew. Me particularly: I have no wish to be a monument to your pique.'

'Of course, you're there. Well that's something on the credit side.'

'Thank you very much.'

'That's all right. I pay these thoughtful compliments all the time. Move on, it's later than you think.'

Captain Bradley Heald, balding, square built, had been grounded now for over twelve months. This would be a last trip before retirement from active space service. He had known for some years that he would not get an independent command and this last mission was in some ways exactly suited to his capacities. Final authority rested in someone else and all the routine matters of a straightforward run for his attention. He could have been grateful; because it would add space time to his service book and make a difference to the retirement terms which would soon be offered. But no-one is grateful for being accurately judged, and he reserved the right to say, 'It's a bloody one-man band in this Corporation. What does Fletcher think he's doing? I could take this flight myself. X is a pleasure cruiser, handles itself. Six trainees. That's work for the executives. Watch and watch, I shouldn't wonder. Cape Horn stuff. Senior Controllers, my arse.'

The chosen confidant for this fundamental *exposé* was Stuart Marsh, power executive, no less. He was inclined to agree. Iron grey hair, walking with a limp from an old crash injury, his special aim was to put in enough missions to take an early retirement on full pension and then work in his own lab on fuel research projects. Even giving half his mind to the job, he was an outstandingly good engineer and Fletcher knew that Power was still all right if the two trainees proved completely U.S.; but he was also aware that his power number one offered a management problem.

None of this democratic urge to knock the government was in evidence when Fletcher called his first briefing. Since it was a dual or even treble purpose flight, he took it in the command cabin of *Interstellar X.*

In the confined space, his new team looked more like a group of casual sightseers, crammed in to listen to the guide give a run down on a historical monument. He had felt that before, at the beginning of a mission, and knew that in the long months ahead, even with time rationalisation, these strangers would become as well known to each other as their own faces in a mirror. The psychological and physiological insult of living at this density could only be borne by a willingness to sink individualism in a community will. Either it happened or the mission was a grinding agony. It had always happened, so far, for him as a Commander; but ships had come back with half their crew unfit for further space service, far gone on the road of mental deterioration.

Vernon Spencer's sardonic, dark, thin face arrested his

attention in mid period. The crew man had posted himself
away from the navigation group and was sharing the narrow
cradle of the communication's console with the communication's executive, Tamar Kelly. She was sitting, chin on
hand, with her spectacular, elastic bell of red gold hair swung
forward like a personal acoustic cowl. Spencer was totally
absorbed in following its shining, asymptotic curve with two
lightly touching fingers. It was the mathematics of it that
interested him primarily; though nobody, however intellectu-
ally given, could sit so close to Tamar Kelly without being
aware that there was more to it than mathematical form.

Dag said equably, 'Spencer. Your life and unfortunately
mine might well depend on your familiarity with these details.
Channel your familiarity this way.'

Spencer was all polite compliance, 'Certainly Commander
I can continue this piece of research at a more convenient
time. I am all attention.'

'I'm glad of that. To give you every aid to concentration,
move now to the navigation console and follow it through
with your executive.'

Again it was said without heat, but this time in a voice
which left no room for repartee. Spencer was in fact half way.
across, edging a way through the pack, before he realised
he had been instinctively obedient. 'All right then, Fletcher,'
he said, wisely to himself, 'I'll watch that. You won't move
me so easily again.'

Dag Fletcher went on with his exposition and at the same
time wondered if he would have bothered to move Spencer
if it had been anyone but Tamar Kelly. He had to admit that
she meant a good deal more to his peace of mind than he had
ever intended that she should. Frank, golden brown eyes
were watching him with a flattering kind of total concentration. It was a big responsibility to have a girl think you
could do no wrong.

For the first time he had a moment's uncertainty about the
mission. If Spencer was just another awkward crewman, he

could deal with it, as he had done many times before. There was always one who took some special care before he accepted the rigours of the service. But if he was going to try for Tamar it was another matter. He knew that, ridiculous though it might be, he would be jealous as hell.

A similar impatience with events was simmering under the rococo façade of Jacqueline Ann Roth, following the ploy from her vantage point on the power console. She scribbled on a memo tablet and posted it in the breast pocket of Spencer's fatigue suit as he pushed past. When he reached journey's end, he dug it out and read, 'Careful V; she belongs to Daddy.'

Now he looked at Tamar Kelly again. Pale skin, compact, proportionate, in a ribbed turquoise inner suit which fitted like a sheath and flattered trim wrists and ankles. So, Fletcher could be needled that way? It would be a double pleasure.

At the end of the session, Dag brought in his Co-Pilot. 'Have you anything to say, Captain Heald?'

Heald's delivery was pure ham; but he covered the ground without missing a detail. He ended 'Lift off 1430 then. Check out from 1400. That means everyone inside and sealed up. This isn't a mock-up with beer and skittles waiting in the mess, it's for real. Say your goodbyes early and get here with a steady hand. That's all I have, Commander. With your permission I'll give the stand down.' Then he was following his crew down the ramps of the silent ship to the loading bay where the service hoist was still bringing up the last stores.

Tamar Kelly came down at the end of the line with Fletcher.

'What's bothering this Spencer, Dag?'

'Something for sure. He's clever enough. Why would he play stupid?'

'Could be a reluctant space man. Family pressure this way and some other secret passion.'

'Perhaps you could find out.'

'I could try if you want me to. But he's not my type.'

That should have satisfied him. But he was driven against his better judgement to add, 'Work on it then.'

'Office hours only?'

'Whenever the spirit moves you, of course.'

Warm brown eyes had a speculative look. 'Dag. You're jealous.'

He was suddenly ashamed of himself and stopped in the narrow aisle. They were out of any recognisable world in the sloping gun metal tube. A limbo, where her warm lips were as unexpected as if he was touching them for the first time. He said, 'Sorry, Tamar. I still only half believe it. You have to remind me every now and again.'

'Like this?'

'Just like that.'

In spite of the years of command and the success in his chosen field of work, Fletcher had still some areas of uncertainty. It meant that he took nothing for granted and Tamar, had she thought, could have told him that it made a part of his considerable charm.

For blast-off, Fletcher brought all personnel except one into the command cabin. It was tight, but not unmanageable. In full service, the corvette would carry nine, at action stations, in the space. Bringing in another cradle, left only one outside—at the auxiliary power console in the power pack itself. Marsh had quickly sized up his two assistants. The massive, black-bearded Don Voller was hunched beside him at the main console. It was the girl, Roth, who was on detachment below. She had already shown a natural grasp of the facts of life in a real set-up.

Technicians in the blockhouse, visible on the scanner, signalled the last rites and Dag prepared to pull the plug. Even now, he could not go through this routine without a rising excitement. It was all beginning again. It was like moving out of life into a new medium where anything could happen.

Consciously, without the filter of physical death, whatever that did. Leaving a known, predictable world where human psychology had prepared itself over the ages to deal with a particular set of environmental factors and moving into a different sphere, where other criteria were determinants, where the totally strange could be the norm.

To him, the beginning was always satisfying. Vibration was building up, tangible even through the foam shock cradles and the pressurised suits. He listened to the round-up of reports from the consoles. Bruce Charlton, matter of fact from Navigation, 'All systems Go.'

Stuart Marsh, gravel voiced, 'Power. All systems Go.'

Tamar, deep husky contralto, 'Communications. All systems Go.'

Then, as though he had not heard it for himself, Heald reporting in to him, 'Co-Pilot to Commander. All systems Go.'

Dag said, 'Hear this, all. Good luck on this mission. Counting down now.' He pushed home the red firing pin and *Interstellar X* was a fused bomb. No power on Earth could keep it back. Ten seconds later she was lifting from the pad. A slow, graceful, silver pointer, with an orange fire ball beating down on gantry and blockhouse in an intolerable back-wash of thermal agitation.

Two hours later, on course, with the corvette settled in a fantastic, space-consuming stride, Fletcher said, 'Stand down. Minimum watch, Captain, if you please.'

Mimicking the voice, but switched off the net and on a direct link to Tamar Kelly, Spencer said, 'The question is who will watch minimum?'

She said, 'Clear the line, Spencer, and get back on net. Don't do that again unless there's a direct instruction to scramble.'

'There was.'

'Since when have you been number one?'

Heald's voice overrode their link and drowned out Spencer's

reply. 'Communications Executive and Navigation Three take first watch. I'll have the details of the rest posted within the hour. Stand down all.'

Fletcher thought, 'Damn Heald, he's given Tamar the most awkward detail on the list.' He was about to intervene on their personal link, when the complications of such an intervention became clear to him. Of course, it would have to stand. On any one of a number of counts. It was Heald's business to run the ship. Any suggestion of favouritism would be wholly bad. It would appear to Tamar that he did not trust her. It would appear to Spencer that he was afraid of competition from him.

Except in technical, professional matters, where his computer mind dropped out the considered answer like a robot mechanism, he was given to this invalidating over-think. The moment, anyway, when an intervention could have appeared spontaneous and purely businesslike was long gone. So he chalked up a small count of dissatisfaction and switched through the personal monitor to his day cabin. Then he was following Heald out of the control room.

The two remaining residents felt the relief of freedom to move. Tamar broke out helmet seals and hinged back her visor. Then she shook her head, like a spaniel out of water, clearing the fine clinging hair into its unique, bell-shaped curve. When she joined Spencer at the navigation console, he was already digging down into an inner pouch for a pack of cigarettes.

'Smoke?'

'Not now. Nor you.'

He looked at her in genuine astonishment. 'Oh, come on now. What's this? What can there be possibly wrong with a smoke after three hours in these sardine cans?'

'Nothing at all, except in here. On a duty stint there is a definite and categorical regulation. Smoking on watch details is *out*.'

He went on, tapping out a cigarette from the full pack

with pleasurable deliberation. When it was between his lips, he snapped on a small blow torch from the standard belt equipment of his suit. Then he blew a long thin jet of smoke at the centre of the scanner screen, where a plate-sized Earth shone whitely through the instant smog.

'Put it out, Spencer.'

'Or what? You'll tell Daddy all about it?' He was enjoying himself. This one riled easily. He looked appreciatively at the high colour already swamping out a small patch of freckles across the bridge of her nose.

Tamar Kelly reached above her head to a rack of small metal bottles in the low roof. She realised that this issue had to be settled at the outset. Promotion to executive rank had been quick for her, technical competence had done that. Command experience was short weighted; but under the volatile nature was a cool instinctive knowledge of some basic facts of life. One such was very clear to her. There could only be one person in charge at a time.

She consciously steeled herself for a showdown, biting inside her lower lip to stop a small tremor. Before he realised what she was doing, he was cocooned in plastic foam. She said evenly, 'I'm calling in Freya Burleigh to replace you for ten minutes. Get cleaned up and be back in time or you'll spend the rest of the watch in the brig.'

He was unexpectedly quiet, 'All right, Ginger, you've made your point. That's game to you. But don't do anything like that again or I just might loosen a few of those pretty teeth. I wouldn't like to have to do that to a Lieutenant.'

'This time I'll ignore that.'

When he had shuffled out, leaving an elephant spoor of grey blobs, she felt sick with reaction. There was also an unwilling interest. How did anyone get to be so damned awkward? What made him tick? She remembered also, very dark, very angry eyes glaring at her, and had to accept the unpalatable fact that she was even slightly afraid of him.

In ten days (Rationalised Time), *Interstellar* X had a crew. Basic adjustments to a specially compact kind of community life had been made; some willingly, some reserving intention to opt out as and when opportunity knocked. On Day 15 (RT) Fletcher ran through the approach drill for Fingalna. When he asked for questions, Spencer asked, 'Will there be any shore leave?'

'Go through the drill, Navigation Three, as I laid it on.'

Vernon Spencer fixed an enigmatic eye on Tamar Kelly and reeled off the precise and exact routine as expounded and finished in the same tone with his original question.

'I'm glad you have enough sense to give your mind to this. It's a navigation job mainly. Once communications have given you the green light it's up to you to get her on the pad without making a tunnelling bid.' Dag registered the direction of the fixed speculative gaze of Spencer's eyes and had to damp down a rising irritation. 'I'll answer your leave query. There will be forty-eight hours for refuelling and maintenance. Security demands six crew on board. Captain Heald will work out a relief rota. It should give a few hours each. Watch the local wine, it's true snakesweat.'

Fingalna was football size on the scanner and coming up fast. When they left the briefing it was to seal up and make for action stations. Jacqueline Ann Roth followed Spencer out. She had watched his preoccupation with Tamar without any enthusiasm. 'Give me a hand, V. I've got a zip I can't reach. Unless, of course, your lush lieutenant has prior claims.'

Like others who fish for compliments she pulled in a catch which was only worth throwing back.

'She hasn't yet, but she will have; until then I might as well keep my hand in.'

Landing was copybook. *Interstellar* X flamed down out of a clear sky and dropped to its designated pad with such finely calculated retro that it did not sink to the full depth of its hydraulic rams. Then it rose slowly to its towering height as a mobile gantry ran up to damp the heat with clouds of dense grey gas.

Dag Fletcher, observing protocol, dressed in his I.G.O. uniform of full commander and was first ashore with Tamar Kelly in the ceremonial green and gold tabard of the service. A hovering tender took them from the high entry port and flashed like a dragonfly to the Reception Centre. Routine registration of flight details was quicker than he had ever known it. He picked up details of the passengers who were to come aboard. Then he took Tamar to the Space Port Grill.

'All we can do this trip. I'm afraid we can't stay tonight. I'll need to be aboard to check out take-off patterns.'

'Can you tell me where?'

'No. But to save any Delilah syndrome I might add that I don't know myself.'

'Oh good. That saves my face. I wouldn't like to think I couldn't make you tell all. Now I don't have to try.'

'How are you getting on with Spencer?'

'No progress; but give me time.'

For the first time since he had known her, she did not look directly at him. It was, in fact, not a successful meal. The restaurant could have been anywhere in the Galaxy. Standard equipment, poised on a slender stalk overlooking the space port, only the small silvery Fingalnians and a greenish quality in the light from the panoramic windows gave a clue that they were out of Europe, Earth. Both were in some way relieved to have the activity of getting a shuttle back to the ship.

Heald met them at the port. 'I thought it would be you returning, Commander. Our passengers have arrived. There's a small problem. Dr. Tancred's assistant is a woman. It makes an accommodation change. Executive Kelly has the only double cabin. She will have to go in there. But perhaps one of the juniors should share it and give up a single.

'No, that will be all right. Leave the executive in there.'

In an obscure way, he was glad. He did not drag it out into full daylight, but the thought that she was not alone was satisfactory. It meant certainly that she was not easily accessible to anyone except himself.

He went to his day cabin which doubled as reception area when in port and sent Don Voller to round up the newcomers and bring them in to be introduced. Their folders were on his desk and he had flipped through Dr. Tancred's when Voller ushered them in.

Cormac, a Venusian, the I.G.O. commissar was first. Almost as wide as the hatch. Small, broad; hooded, triangular eyes; voice, however, very forthright and giving the lie to any aura of menace he might project. Dr. Tancred followed him; pale skin and silver hair of the Fingalnian ethnological stock, a round jolly looking type, smiling as a habit. Voice flat and metallic, at odds with the Cherible Brother exterior.

Then the tail-end Charley of the procession stole the show and made the routine of introductions suddenly less of a chore. Dr. Tancred's assistant was a small vibrant figure, less than five feet tall. She was a platinum blonde, with pale green eyes and a skin of white alabaster. Wearing a sleeveless tunic of fine transparent linen in the Fingalnian style and a short heavily pleated skirt of the same colour as her eyes. Exact classical proportions carried out in the satisfying oval of the face and in the architecture of the body. Seven heads tall, a head width between jewelled points of well separated breasts. Head depth from breasts to navel. Moving like shining quicksilver. Voice clear and metallic saying, 'How do you do, Commander. Captain Bwadley has given me a lovely woom. I'm certain we'll have a lovely time together. I'm Vanowa.'

It was a good half hour before an indignant Tamar burst into the day cabin. 'Dag, did you have anything to do with putting that little silver creep in my cabin?'

'Steady now. She looks a nice girl. You'll get on well together.'

'So you did. Thank you very much. She makes me feel like a lumbering great cow. And she's practically filled the place with equipment. I don't like her and I tell you there's something phoney about her. Why did you do it? Never mind. I can see you had some twisted reason. And I think I know what it was.'

Before he could speak, she had gone.

He heard her saying, 'Voller, would you find Spencer for me. Tell him I'd like a word with him in the Command cabin.'

CHAPTER TWO

FOUR days out from Fingalna, on a trajectory which, if unchecked, would put *Interstellar* X on an elliptical orbit round Cappodan, Dag Fletcher signed himself in for a timed entry on the log. 'Day 20 (RT) 1200 hours. Commander. In accordance with instructions, opening sealed navigational orders at this time.' He gave the stellar fix and then spun a dial in his office safe to reach a slim green envelope which contained course data for Thirza. When he had it, there was not much to dictate. Three lines of digits and references to feed into his computers and a short paragraph. Tamar Kelly would have to break it down into precise information for the navigators.

He took it slowly giving a one-second pause between each item. Making an indelible record on the master log. Should there be any inquiry, at a later date, this copy of the orders would be taken as the official version. That meant that a second executive officer should witness its authenticity. Heald was the obvious choice and Fletcher's hand was stretching out for the intercom when he heard the slightest hint of a metallic click from the narrow corridor outside his door.

Once motivated, he worked at an instinctive level. He resumed dictation of the second part of the memo which defined required action on Thirza and detailed the steps to be taken in setting up an official consulate there. Meanwhile, he left the desk and circled round to the hatch. Instinct had moved him, but his mind was telling him that he was making a fool of himself. It was a peaceful mission; the crew prob-

24

lems he had, raised no loyalty issues. Not planetary loyalties anyway.

With a hand gripping the release catch, he also told himself that he had gone the wrong way about it. He should have switched the log to repeat. Then he could have moved without the change of location of voice. But it was too late to bother. Anyone with a listening device would know that he had moved towards the door.

With the catch eased off, he threw it back in a smooth surge of force that made its disappearance look like a sleight of hand trick. He appeared to replace its blank grey surface with his own chest and Vanora, very politely, knocked twice on his sternum. She looked, as usual, as though the mere sight of him was a considerable pleasure in itself and said with disarming simplicity, 'Please may I talk to you, Commander?'

He said, 'Come in and tell me all,' standing aside. There was not much room, but she made it appear even less and brushed closely past. Any electronic listening aid she carried would have to be very small to be concealed on that trim figure. She was in a plain silvery inner suit, which was cloudy rather than opaque. The gag, 'Every silver lining has its cloud' rose to his mind, but he manfully kept it out of overt speech. In the confined space of the small cabin, she put in as valid a claim to notice as an incendiary bomb. Whatever scent she was wearing was unfamiliar to him, but was entirely at odds with formal conversation.

He said, 'You will be glad to know that I now have course directions for our objective. As soon as we have it translated into navigational detail I shall be able to tell you how long it will take.'

'You have such a happy ship, Commander, I don't care how long it takes.'

'That's very kind of you to say so; but others will no doubt want to get on with the mission. What can I do for you, anyway?'

Even as he said it, he knew it was a stupid way to put the

question and Vanora's wide open green eyes gave a clear signal that she would be delighted to fill out a blank cheque. He said hastily, 'What did you want to talk to me about?'

'How business-like you are Commander. I suppose you are so interested in that lovely *wed* girl, that you can't see anybody else at all?' She had now moved round his desk and was standing beside the chair to which he had returned. Having lost the managerial advantage of facing her across the desk top, he swivelled to face her and at the same time dropped the I.G.O. letter into a filing slot.

'Don't you twust me?'

'It's not a question of "twust". Security drill is an obligatory thing. What's on your mind?'

This again was so obvious that it made no contribution at all to progress. She said, 'I just wanted to talk to you about the end part of the mission.' Spoken by Vanora the words seemed just precocious nonsense, as though a very beautiful child was playing a grown-up game. 'I know I took it on with my eyes open. But I don't think I want to stay on the planet with Dr. Tancwed. Can you ovewule the memo and take me back with you?'

She was so close to the chair that her thighs were touching the side of his leg and he could feel warmth and a light, pneumatic pressure. Fingalnians, in spite of their pallor, had a normal blood heat of thirty-nine degrees centigrade. It was as unexpected, in a reverse sense, as the coldness of a warmly coloured snake.

There was a quick tap at the hatch. It slid back and Tamar Kelly was well inside before the tableau made any special impression on her. Vanora had reacted as though she were steadying herself and had put one hand on the lapel of his short-sleeved service tunic. Tamar said, icily for her, 'Oh, I see. You have your hands full. I'll come back when you can spare the time.'

'It shouldn't take long.'

'I can well believe that.'

Dag felt it to be a ridiculous situation and was totally disinclined to do anything about it. He said evenly, 'I'll ring you in about five minutes. Which cabin are you likely to be in?'

'The ward room.'

'Very well. Would you be so good as to pass the word for Captain Heald to look in here as soon as it is convenient?'

'Certainly.'

A brusque turn away, which sent the red gold elastic bell surging round in a shock wave and she was gone.

He said, 'Vanora, let's get this straight. I'm a regulations' man. Whatever interest I have in Executive Kelly, I save for shore leave and that goes for any other woman member of this crew. For your private record, I think you are very beautiful. That's the lot. Now we'll deal with your request and you can go and sit on the other chair.'

For a long five seconds Vanora looked steadily into his eyes. Her own were wide open, pale green, luminous. Then she went obediently round the table.

When she left the office, minutes later, he was not at all convinced that she had come with that request at first. It could be quick thinking on her part and a possible try on to see how he would react. He had promised to take it up with Cormac and see what could be done. She paused at the door and stood in a classical *déhanchement* to fire the Parthian shot. 'If you should *want* me Commander, just give a wing on that clever intercom.'

Then she was moving out of the way to let Heald bustle in. Fletcher waited until she was clear, then checked back his log entry, with Heald following the original. Somehow, they had not got down to Christian name familiarity which was unusual with Dag. He said, 'Do you agree with that, Captain?'

Heald was equally formal. 'Certainly, Commander, and I'm glad to see it. This means a change of course as soon as the details are cleared.'

'Yes. Call action stations and I'll put Lieutenant Kelly to work.'

'I'll take it along to her myself. Stations in ten minutes?'

'Check.'

Alarm bleeps sounding through the ship at 1230 hours brought some willing and some unwilling to the command centre. Vanora was coming out of the Power executive's cabin when Tamar Kelly went past at a clumsy trot with only her visor to seal. Tamar slowed, was about to speak, thought better of it, and hurried on. Never before given much to vindictive musing, she could not help thinking that if Vanora could be kept in a spacesuit it would be an all-round advantage.

It was as well that she could not see the expression that followed her down the narrow way. Although there was no change in the pale, oval face. Vanora's green eyes had a malevolent glitter which would have alarmed her. The look transformed the Fingalnian. She was no longer a slight, almost childlike figure; but adult, intelligent and extremely dangerous. Stuart Marsh, however, saw none of that when she turned back into his door and said, 'Oh good, that wed girl has gone. You can come and help me to get dwessed up.'

The bleeps held on for three minutes and then stopped, creating a silence which was suddenly tense and expectant. Marsh was last into the control room and earned himself an irritable request from Heald.

'For God's sake, Power One, give me clearance. If this wasn't R.T. we'd go grey waiting for you.'

He ran a rapid check over his console and spoke to Jacqueline Ann on her lonely outpost.

'Power. All systems Go.'

When Fletcher received the collected clearance, he did a personal check on his three passengers. Dr. Tancred and Cormac had been given couches in the wardroom. Vanora was using one of the dual purpose bunks in her own cabin.

Tancred checked in his polite, unemotional fashion, Cormac grudgingly, as though registering that these affairs were only conducted with any efficiency in the Venusian fleets. From Vanora, there was no answer. It would be just like the image she had established of herself, to find that she appeared in the hatch with some naïve query, when the course change was building its fantastic G. If that did happen it would be the last question she would ever utter.

It was the first time in a long experience that Fletcher had ever held back a major flight order for such a reason. He said wearily, 'Navigation Two. Quickly please. Dig yourself out and check on Vanora.'

Freya Burleigh's plummy contralto was saying correctly, 'Navigation Two. Check on Vanora. Moving now, Commander,' when the Fingalnian girl came on the net herself.

'I've been having a dwedful stwuggle, with these stwaps. All set now Commander. You can do anything you like.'

Marsh looked quickly round the cabin. He knew that when he left she had been settled in the couch. What had she been doing in the interim? What anyway could she do? Nothing obviously that could matter. And any intervention would only involve himself in what might be thought to be a ludicrous reason for his own lateness. He looked back at his console and said nothing.

Fletcher, taking it on manual, said, 'Stand by for major course change. Counting down now.' He watched a sweep hand eat its way through the red quadrant and he hit the precise micro second with 'Retro.'

Interstellar X pivotted on her heel and a racing maze of stars wheeled past the direct vision port. Fletcher was giving out his navigational instructions like a computer. He *was* a computer, an extension of the electronic brains of his ship. It was a performance that the trainees would be lucky to see again. A totally efficient and experienced pilot putting a fine ship through her paces. Most commanders would have been more than content to hold a watching brief, whilst the mechanical brains took control. But this way, the sense of human direction was emphasised. It brought out the best in the crew. Every instruction went through with a sense of shared satisfaction that human minds could use this power and dominate this inhuman environment.

Then she was away again. Dead on the new course, clawing back to a space-consuming velocity which would take them through the maze of stars on this rim of the Galaxy, to the tiny distant planet Thirza, known so far, only as a spectrogram on an I.G.O. file.

Stand down came with a sense of anticlimax, as though there should have been more of the personal contact with flight problems, before they settled down again to the routine, featureless slog. Fletcher stayed at his console to look at the new flight plan which the computers had set up. Bruce Charlton remained for a duty spell as executive officer and Jacqueline Ann came in from her outpost as general dogsbody.

She had called in home on the way and dumped space gear. But she had not stayed to change out of a deep pink undersuit which gave the simple and pleasing effect of having stepped out of a bath of pink dye. She went straight to Fletcher and he reflected that by and large he had certainly got himself a decorative crew.

'Commander.'

'Here, present.'

'I heard the fuss on about Vanora. I think she was looking for you. She was going into the admin. office when I went down to my bolt hole.'

'Thank you. I'll check on that. See if there was anything she wanted.'

Jacqueline Ann hoped that she had put Vanora in a spot. Her move had not been pure altruism. She had noticed that Vanora was interesting herself in Spencer amongst others, and any little she could do to bring grief into that silvery life would be pure pleasure.

It was not as easy as all that, however. She was not immediately to be found. Working methodically, she had got round to Bradley Heald and was finding a more encouraging welcome. This time, she had struck the right note by telling him how much she appreciated the smooth running of the ship and what a good commander of it he would be. It was not put in so many words but it was clear enough and coupled with the suggestion that she really preferred, mature, older men, it secured her as good a press as could be got from anyone who could only, basically, be interested in himself.

Vanora was sure that she knew her man. It had not taken her long to size up the ship's company. Fletcher she had tried, but without any real hope of success. It would have been very simple if she could have influenced him. But next best was Heald, then Stuart Marsh. Vernon Spencer and Don Voller were also possible targets. Spencer was obviously against the government and a law to himself. Voller had a natural bent for lotus eating. He would not be numbered in any roll call of those 'whose shoulders held the sky suspended'. If she could make a group out of the four with a common interest, even if in the first instance it had to be done at a personal level, she could go ahead with phase two which was to reveal how self interest could be served.

The mission of *Interstellar X* was known even before Fletcher had accepted it. The I.G.O. Central Research Bureau had been penetrated by O.G.A. intelligence for many years. It was, in the long run, cheaper than running a big research programme for the Outer Alliance on an independent basis. Very few new finds came up. Mostly routine investigations added detail to the stellar chart, so many more identified and named planetary systems. So many more empty and valueless lumps of matter noted and given a stellar fix. But just occasionally something came up which made it worth while.

Trained agents might wait for many years living normal lives, not used for any other intelligence chore so that their usefulness would not be compromised. One such mission in a lifetime paid the whole retrospective bill.

Vanora had trained and then qualified normally as a geologist. She was a good one and had been very successful as Tancred's assistant on a dozen normal assignments. Now the situation she had been prepared for had developed. It was a once only job. Afterwards she would have to retire with no further value as an agent of this kind. But when she finally got on to the topic she had been aiming at, there was no hint in her voice of the importance to herself of getting the right answer.

'What would you say, Bwadley, if I told you I knew how to make a lot of money?'

Her very warm lips were practically brushing his ear, so it was said clearly; but so quietly that it could be turned as a misconstruction if necessary.

'I'd say you were a very clever girl.'

'What would you do for a lot of money? To spend, say, in Abulion?'

'That's in O.G.A. space.'

'Well, it's a lovely place to live.'

'That I know. What are you getting at Vanora?'

'Suppose I said I could get all this money and a place to live in Abulion. Would it intewest you?'

'What's the catch?'

'No catch, Bwadley. Don't you twust me? If I tell you will you pwomise not to tell anyone else even if you don't agwee? It could get me into sewious twouble.'

'All right.'

'I had an offer just before we set out. O.G.A. are intewested in Thirza. Minewal wights, I think. They want samples and the exact fix. What can it matter to us? It does no one any harm and we get to be vewy wich.'

'That wouldn't be easy.'

Behind his head, she smiled with great satisfaction. It was the right answer. He had not rejected it outright in a spasm of outraged virtue, so he was more than half way home. She was sure of him. It would do to be going on with. Later, when he was committed by action, and there was no way back, she could take it a little further. The big step, that *Interstellar X* and any crew members foolishly possessed of inflexible loyalties would have to be neutralised, would keep for some time. But there was little doubt in her mind that it would have to come to that.

Meanwhile, Fletcher had abandoned a fairly casual search and went into his office to think out, from there, what aim she could possibly have in going in when she knew it would be empty. He had not been greatly helped by his first *confidante*. Looking into the cabin which Vanora shared, he found Tamar Kelly methodically preparing her space kit for the next action call. She was working on the floor and presented a neat, symmetrical, turquoise bottom to the opening hatch.

Only a man of iron would not have given it a fond pat. When, however, having recognised his quick light tread, she said without looking up, 'Oh, come in Vernon,' it started the conversation on a low level of goodwill.

'I'm looking for Vanora.'

'I should try your bed. She might be waiting there with ill concealed impatience.'

He let it pass.

'She was seen going into the office when we were waiting for her to report in. Can you think of any reason why she would want to do that?'

'Not if it was empty.'

'Thank you very much, you're being a big help. I don't have to say this, but just to clear any ideas you might have, I don't care two damns about Vanora.'

It was an olive branch and had cost a little effort to say it; but he was anxious to get back to their footing of easy intimacy and understanding. Like all appeasement, it was not a big success.

'I'm sure I don't care what you think about her.'

All his old lack of certainty in dealing with women returned to him and he withdrew into formality.

'It might be important to know what she is up to. Have you any idea what equipment she brought on board?'

'All normal geological stuff as far as I can tell. You can see there's a lot.'

Flat grey cases were secured in the recessed luggage bays. It would take some time to make a thorough search. Sampling would be quicker and in some ways as useful, since anything incriminating would obviously be well concealed. Not that there was any reason to suppose there was anything to find.

He let his eyes rove round the collection and cleared his mind of any preference for shape or size. When he pointed to a small oblong case in one of the ceiling racks, it was a selection as random as a computer would have made it.

'Open that one for me.'

'Is that official?'

'If you like.'

'It isn't what I like, it's a simple matter of regulations.'

'You don't have to remind me about that. Get it down and open it.'

This time there was no mistake in his voice. She unbuckled the wide straps and lifted the case on to her own couch.

It contained only an item which should be in every well found geologist's portmanteau. For the most part, it held a very snappy line in theodolites, with a small motor, powered by a compact energy cell; so that once set up it responded to push button control. The rest of the jealously used space was filled with spare cells. She would be using it, no doubt, to do a detailed survey of interesting areas. Preparing a grid to submit with the test drilling data and ore samples. It showed the care she and Tancred were preparing to take; because the aerial record of scanner pictures and panoramic views from the scanner, when at rest, would make a fairly close analysis of the terrain.

Working from a general knack of handling complex equipment, Fletcher put it together and tested it out. It seemed a very satisfactory instrument, but the power element puzzled him. Manual adjustment would have been good enough and not asking much from its operator. Power operation introduced a much higher failure possibility and was only marginally an advantage. He was looking at it and thinking this when Tamar said, 'Well, now you've seen it, don't you think it could be put back? Suppose she comes in?'

'That is my problem; but you're right, there is no need to make an unnecessary fuss. Well, you see how it goes together, just pack it away. I'll keep her out of the way for the next ten minutes. Don't mention to her that we've had it out.'

'She hardly ever speaks to me. I'm the wrong sex. Your little friend only has one idea in her head.'

'One good idea is all anybody needs.'

She was suddenly contrite and turned to the door saying, 'Dag, I'm . . .' but he had already gone.

Something about the apparatus she was handling was more familiar than it had any right to be. She had returned to the only clear piece of the floor space and was telescoping the legs back into the thick base plate which carried its own miniature console. The angle of the legs adjusted on a ratchet and small wear marks showed which position had been most used. Set there, the slender tubular supports looked like antennae. She checked the angle. Proving nothing perhaps, other than the long arm of coincidence, it would be perfect as a special dipole arrangement for receiving on 1420.

Steps outside reminded her that she should hurry. Dag ought to be told of the possibility, but it could wait. Anyway, she could watch herself for any sign that Vanora made unusual use of this equipment. Certainly, so far, it had not been out of its box before this time. Whoever was in the corridor went on past the door. It sounded like Freya Burleigh. She lifted the heavy case back into its niche and strapped it down.

When it was done, she stood for a moment and flipped back the port cover for direct vision into space. It was still exciting to her to see the interstellar night and its strange silent life. Mathematics was her professional tool and still an absorbing interest. The galaxy to her was like a structural bodying forth of its principles. Neither cold nor inhospitable, but an extension of mind. But the aesthetics of it touched the more generalised emotional person, which was never far below the surface in Tamar Kelly. She thought, 'I'm being a simple bitch with Dag. I'd better go and make peace with him. Life's too short to spend any part of it at cross purposes.'

He liked to see her in plain white, with a head band flattening her hair and emphasising the satisfying proportions of her full oval face. She always told him that any psychoanalyst would draw very nasty conclusions from this; but just now she wanted to please and made a quick change. When she left the cabin, she was actually humming a tune—a living testament to the adage that we best please ourselves when we aim to please others.

Ultimate proof that it was sound thinking was, however, hard to come by; the object of the exercise seemed to have disappeared. Used to the layout of the normal freight and passenger ships of the fleet, she did not look in the one place where *Interstellar X* differed from the civilian pattern.

Dag Fletcher had paused in his search for Vanora, reflecting that she could not very well leave the ship and must come up for air sometime. He had gone forward into the cone to the small gunnery control capsule which lay beyond the hydroponic tank section and carried the direct firing equipment for the ship's principle armament.

In military service, the capsule would always be manned. Remote control of the heavy calibre lasers was vested in the command cabin, but, for fighting the ship, nothing could replace the personal direction of a gunnery officer with open, all round vision from a gimbal-mounted couch.

Dag operated the console and gave himself maximum vision. Then he swivelled round, methodically searching the immense vistas of hurrying stars in sweeping, 360° circuits. He did not precisely know why he was doing it, or what he expected to see; but he had acted on illogical insight before and now never disregarded it. No man could spend the time he had spent in the wastelands of space, without giving value to the imponderables of random thought and the influence of events approaching through the screens of time.

On the final swing, he was looking back along the new course. Cutting above and below its basic line, using remote reflecting gear to avoid the slowly gyrating silver tube which was the ship. He had himself brought up an I.G.O. corvette to within blasting distance of an enemy frigate on such a line from astern. Where would he lie to be an unobtrusive tail? There. Yes, about there. Dead astern in the blind spot for a civilian ship. And there was a star there.

Bruce Charlton saw an unfamiliar panel of his console come to life with some surprise. It was short lived. His commander came up life-size on the central screen. 'Bruce, I'm in the gunnery turret. Give me the console on remote and sit in on this. Pass the word to your assistant. Who is it?'

'Jacqueline Ann.'

'Of course. Pass the word to her that this is a matter for the confidential log and explain what that means.'

Jacqueline Ann Roth was already pinkly present and spoke for herself. 'I heard that, Commander. I understand.'

'Good. Let's go then.'

It was really a communications' job. But Fletcher never bothered much about section susceptibilities and with the possible exception of Tamar Kelly could handle this chore better than anyone on the ship. He was working under some difficulty with the restricted panel in the turret, but what he lost in refinement was compensated by the 'feel' of operating with direct vision. Slowly he beamed in on the distant star. Patiently, moving in micro-second adjustments, he began to build a picture on the grid screen which filled a wall of the command cabin and was relayed to him in a small clear replica.

It was nearer than any star that size could be. There was almost no time lag on the return of his probing beams. It was a small perfect circle and then plainly a cone with its apex pointing their way. That was as far as definition could go, and the grain was so coarse that blowing it up would not give much greater clarity. He knew they were in trouble. The statistical likelihood of another ship being just there by chance was too great to give it a thought.

He said, 'Well, there you have it, Bruce. We won't get his houseflag, but I'll guarantee that it's O.G.A. Blow it up and get me the biggest, clearest still you can. I'll be with you in a few minutes.'

On the way back, he thought it out. By some means they had been picked up out of Fingalna and followed. Not too difficult at that when you came to think. But it immediately raised the point that it was known then that they were on a special mission. Where was the leakage? Somewhere in Fingalna? Tancred and Vanora; that was more likely than the dour Cormac. I.G.O. officials were hand-picked from the galaxy for a long, safe record of reliability. Could be Earth Terminal. Not somehow as likely though; because not many people could have known. Unless the I.G.O. link itself had been penetrated. But he had only picked the crew himself just before the flight. It would be too dodgy to plant an agent that way. There did not in fact have to be an agent; it was just knowledge of *Interstellar X*'s destination. The rest could be a simple job of cross bearings and picking up the course. That argued a big operation with more than one ship. Others out of sight then, keeping him in position by cross reference? That was not a comfortable thought.

He arrived at the command cabin as Bruce Charlton completed a large full wall-size version of the object on their tail. A communications expert would have done a little better, but it was very good. There was not much doubt about what it was.

Dag said, 'Good work, Bruce, you've done well with that. Do you recognise it?'

'It's a nose cone for sure. But what of? Debris? There's a fair amount of rubbish out here on the rim.'

'No, it's powered. It's on this course. Locked on with mathematical precision. It's a frigate. If it chooses it can come up at a rate that would make us look stupid. And it could turn us into molecular scrap before it was in range of our armament.'

'But why should they want to do that? This is a peaceful ship on business cleared by I.G.O. in I.G.O. space. No planetary fleet would interfere. They'd be afraid of reprisals.'

'How far away is the nearest I.G.O. squadron?'

'I see what you mean. It would take a long time to get anything here. We could be avenged; but who wants to be avenged?'

'Very quick.'

'So what do we do?'

Dag thought again and killed the picture. He told the log that there was a frigate pacing them and gave his account of possibilities. So it was on record. But only for as long as the log itself retained its familiar structural form. Even a skilled investigator would have a job to pick up any thread from the interstellar dust they could easily become.

'We do nothing just now. I don't want any word of this spread round the ship. We are one jump ahead in knowing that she's there. They won't expect that we know. I have a personal code for corporation messages to our own H.Q. I can send something that way. I'll work on it. Meanwhile we confirm that we are being followed. Another course change will do that. There's more than one planet in the solar system with Thirza. Look it up on the charts, pick any one and get some figures out. We can call it a training exercise. Then tomorrow we'll get back on the right one.'

'Check.'

On the way to his cabin, Dag reflected that in Bruce
Charlton, he had the best of his crew, from the point of view
of accepting a situation in the same spirit as he did himself.
By this time, he was usually on Christian name terms with
all the senior men; but this trip there was only Charlton he
could comfortably address in this way.

Two paces from his own door, Tamar came out of it. It
was her second visit, on a repeat circular tour of the ship.
Some of the first enthusiasm for being totally obliging had
rubbed off and she was beginning to feel that she was selling
out the feminist club. This was carried a long step further
by his reaction. Preoccupation with the new facts about the
mission, could not stop him noticing that she looked particularly attractive; but it blunted the impact. Instead of telling
her about it, he said, 'I'll give you advance warning so that
you can make a start. There's a major course change coming
up. About five minutes. See Vanora strapped in before you
leave.'

'But of course, we can't have her spread all over the cabin
wall. After all I have to live in it. Although, I don't know,
I think I could learn to like it. There would be so much
gain.'

She was gone before he could reply and he went inside to
work out a personal message to Paul V. Spencer which would
outline the complications so far. Anything directly to I.G.O.
would be intercepted by the following ship and no code devised
could resist the sort of attention it would get. But something
so simple that there was no reason to expect it to be anything
else might just get away with it.

When urgent bleeps began to sound through the ship to
show that Charlton was ready for course change, he had it
ready. Personal messages went out often enough and would
cause no surprise if they appeared on the file of a monitoring
agent. He had looked back and continued a previous signal
to Spencer on freight expectation for this leg of their trade

route. He carried it a stage further and referred back to a conversation they had never had. Then he suggested that Spencer look again at the proposed rates as their main competitor was interested and might undercut. The Chairman was nobody's fool. He would pick up the reference and inform I.G.O.

In the control cabin, there was no great enthusiasm for the new call. The bleeps had stopped and personnel were waiting in their cocoons for the next thing. He decided to do a Captain Bligh and make them sweat. Tamar was first to suffer and was told in cold officialese to get off the message which he had prepared in long hand.

When it came up on the glowing display spread of her console she asked if there were any laundry lists he would like to add and got a dusty answer which boiled down to a snub direct. Then he went into the mechanics of course change, treating it as a training exercise, ending with a request for Navigation Three to take charge and make the adjustments.

Spencer responded with a casual 'Check' and without giving himself any time at all to verify computation, began to reel off figures for processing by communications. He sounded very bored and very much as though he was going along with the children in a parlour game. Tamar Kelly shot back directions with her usual precise, professional formality and he began trimming the ship, still casual. Marsh filled his power demands without comment, except to repeat each one as though he wanted to be sure they were on record. G began to build.

Tamar said urgently, 'Commander, check navigation. Those figures can't be right.'

Fletcher was already running parallel calculations and could not follow one leap Spencer had made. But the man's mathematics were not in question. Why had he done that? With G building further into an intolerable, crushing weight, he saw the fallacy and pushed the correction out to Tamar. She had it back in seconds in a voice cracking with strain and the desperate struggle she was making to stay conscious.

Dag said, 'Over to me, Bruce,' and saw Charlton use both hands to push over the switch which gave him control. Then he was fighting for the ship with the seconds of consciousness that remained to him. When finally black night swamped through his mind and his body went slack against his holding straps, *Interstellar X* was spinning and turning in a complicated equiangular spiral dive with a comet tail from motors at full thrust.

CHAPTER THREE

It was lost time. Fletcher never knew how long he was out. *Interstellar X* operated by its own built-in logic and after an abortive attempt to disappear up its own rocket tubes, like the backward flying bird of fable, began to widen its spiral flight in ever increasing circles.

First things in vision were his own hands. Disembodied grabs at the end of corrugated steel grey tubes. When they began to move, he realised they belonged to him and his mind was working at an instinctive level to bring the ship under control. They had gone many thousands of miles, for what such reckoning was worth, in the vacant interstellar places. One of the first thoughts in his reeling brain was that any following ship would be well lost. A whole new set of cross bearings would have to be taken to pick them up again, and that would take time. Meanwhile, he had to find out where they were and reset a course. He settled down to wait with the ship idling along.

Bruce Charlton came up shakily.

'Navigation One. Are you all right, Commander?'

'Glad to hear from you, Bruce. We're set fair. Get that stupid bastard Spencer awake, will you?'

'Spencer awake, check.'

Charlton was able to reach his number three without leaving his couch and twisted an oxygen supply valve to give him a boost. Vernon Spencer surfaced reluctantly into an unequivocally hostile environment. As soon as his eyes flickered, Charlton was battering at his ears with demands for him to report ability to take up his duty role. In the end, he said thickly, with a nausea that he could only just hold, 'Navigation three . . . on . . . net.'

Dag Fletcher watched a count of twenty on the sweep second hand above his head. He wanted to be sure Spencer missed no drop of the draught that was on its way. In the interim, Tamar Kelly came up, slurred but determined, and Stuart Marsh, surly and short. Others were stirring; their reports could wait.

He said, 'Hear this, Spencer, and hear it well. You have just missed wrecking the ship and killing the crew and yourself. How you missed doing it we shall never know. Your carefully nurtured habit of civil insolence will cost you dear in future. It will not be allowed to hazard your colleagues again. You will take care and thought and use the judgement which you surely have or you will be isolated from rationalised time; so that you can mature by age. Now you will work out the course change to bring us back parallel to the course we were on. You have ten minutes to do the preliminary work. I have already done the calculation. If your figures disagree with mine you will work the correction out of R.T. which may cost you five years of your life.'

Even through the filter of the intercom, the cold menace of the voice was unmistakable. By this time, there was a full set on the circuit. Some more fully aware of what was going on than others, but the message was clear. It was becoming clear also that Fletcher's reputation was likely to be founded on fact. Spencer was convinced enough to concentrate his whole mind on the problem he had been set. When he came up with an answer, checked and double checked, he had half a minute to go.

Then Fletcher showed another of the command qualities which had put him where he was. It did not turn Spencer into an instant fan, but it went some way to alleviate the immediate bitterness of the schoolboy lesson. He said, without emphasis, as though nothing had happened, 'Commander to

Navigation Three. I agree your analysis. Set the ship on that course if you please.'

There was an intake of breath which could have been Heald registering disapproval. But Spencer went soberly through the chore. At the end of it, he received the standard acknowledgment. 'Thank you, Navigation Three. Stand down, Captain Heald.'

Two days later Thirza was a green apple-sized blob on the scanner and, as far as Dag Fletcher could tell, the shadowing frigate had not picked up the trail. It was hardly surprising; *Interstellar X* had made a move beyond all logical anticipation. To that extent, Spencer had done a good job; but those who knew it made no effort to share the glad tidings.

Tamar Kelly was in a quiet mood. Usually full of chat; it was noticeable that she went about her duties in silent preoccupation. Up to the course change crisis, she had been only playing at the game of making Dag Fletcher sweat it out. She had known that there was nothing between him and Vanora; but it had made a useful stick to get her own back for his lack of confidence. But just before she blacked out, she had known with telepathic certainty that there was something vitally important on his mind which he was keeping hidden from her and she knew also that some others in the crew were in the secret.

That was humiliating and in the same category was the positive knowledge of the human situation which had come to her in the same instant of time. She had always supposed that a deep human bond, such as she had shared with Dag Fletcher, was the most important single thing in human experience. It had to be, to make sense of the isolation of the individual space and time. No sensitive person could go out on a mission without being aware of the pressure towards despair which intimations of infinity relentlessly imposed. Man, even in his technological triumph, was demonstrably insignificant. Such bleak knowledge could only be borne when shared. But in those few revealing moments, she had known that when the chips were down, there was only oneself. An old marathon song was going on in her head with its bitter climax, 'One is one and all alone and ever more shall be so.'

It was daunting for a romantic to know that it was so. She alternated between consideration of the deeper unease and the more irritating, surface one, of what it was that Dag was withholding from her.

The approach to Thirza did something to put both issues out of mind.

Vanora now had a club membership of three, with one adherent who might join at any time. With some skill, she had Bradley Heald, Stuart Marsh and Don Voller all believing that she was chiefly dependent on their individual support and yet got enough group feeling built up to make a party. Vernon Spencer recognised the existence of a cabal and approved of it, instinctively, as being against the government. He was not taken in by Vanora's lisp, but, as an object, she appealed to him. So visits to the cabin she shared with Tamar had the double pleasure of pleasing himself and possibly annoying Fletcher, who would naturally think, since every action of another is related to the self if it possibly can be, that he was there at Tamar's invitation.

Tamar felt this and was not too happy about it. She simply wanted to return to the old confidential relationship with Dag and was not aiming to widen the gap. Perversely, when he went along to talk to her, having noticed the unusual silence, Spencer pushed back the hatch in response to his tap. Vanora was not visible and nobody explained that Spencer had called in at her request. Dag looked past him to where Tamar was sitting on her acceleration couch in a sky-blue track suit. She had just finished a routine session in the isometric drill lab and was glowing like some kind of beacon. He said, 'Not important. I'll see you again when you're not so busy.' Then he was away and only Spencer looked pleased.

Vanora, with Fingalnian disregard for nudity as anything particularly special, appeared from behind the door
of her tall locker wearing only jewellery and green, flip-flop
sandals. It was as if an alabaster figurine had unexpectedly
stepped off its plinth.

Spencer said, 'You wicked little devil, Vanora, you deliberately stayed behind there so that our revered commander
would think that I was alone with his favourite executive.'

'I notice you didn't tell him the twuth.'

'But then who knows what the "twuth" is? Can you
imagine anyone not wanting to be alone with such a pretty
lieutenant?'

Vanora was secure enough on her own pedestal of beauty
not to mind hearing someone else praised. Sensing at once,
that there was some advantage in sabotage to be gained by
pushing it along, she said, 'Well, I'll leave you to talk to her.'
She was half way through the hatch before he picked her up
and brought her back. 'This is a *European* Space Corporation
ship. You can't wander about like that. When in Rome, you
know. Put a nightie on.'

'Put me down then.'

He did it slowly, very conscious of the warmth of her lightweight body. It was as if she had been built of immensely
strong foam polystyrene, sheathed in white peach skin. Even
Spencer's habitual air of indifference to the weather in the
streets was slightly dented. Luminous green eyes held his in
a long speculative look. He said, 'You're definitely the wrong
shape for Long John Silver.'

This came as a surprise to Vanora, she had a long history
of pleasing most people. 'What shape does he like then?'

'Never mind, dear, just scrub round that one.'

But she was not likely to give up without a complex explanation; she had that kind of mind. He was saved by the
bell. Urgent bleeps summoned one and all to stations. Thirza
was literally within striking distance.

Bradley Heald put them into a low shifting orbit and *Interstellar X* circled the small green planet like a busy spinning spider. There was not a lot to see and no great load of choice in the site for a landfall. Dr. Tancred put in a useful professional gloss on the data gathered by the probing sonar beams. He had been co-opted on to the front bench of the communications' section in place of Les Rooney. Dag always believed in using a visiting expert.

In the event, Tancred was not able to deduce much more from the facts than he would have done himself. Some inert gas in the atmosphere was giving the light its green tint. That was no hardship. Some planets had a corpse light which was a perpetual *memento mori*.

There was a good deal of water. Even the land masses were a filigree of lakes and streams. Heat was fairly uniform at 23/25 Centigrade. It would have been feasible to spend some days in analysis, building up a detailed picture of the planet before making any attempt to land, and, no doubt, Tancred expected that they would do just that; but any time spent moving round in the open, advertised where they were. Dag had not seen the shadowing frigate again and had some hope at least that they had not yet been pinpointed. He was prepared to go in and sort it out from ground level.

He set up a three dimensional still which incorporated two hemisphere projections. It reminded him of a biology lab model of the human brain. Soft, plastic lobes channelled and indented, swimming in pale green liquid. One area on the equatorial belt had a lozenge shape of solid ground bigger than anywhere else. Small though it looked, it would contain many hundreds of square miles.

'Commander to Dr. Tancred. Look at grid reference G53 T90.'

Tancred's voice, clipped and metallic, came up intelligently with 'G53 T90, check.'

'Will that suit you as a base?'

'Really, Commander, I had expected more time to make

a careful selection. A good deal will depend on our choice of site.'

'I want the ship down as soon as I can get it. There may be damage from our recent misadventure. You will have to decide now.'

'Very well. It seems to offer the best prospect. But I would have preferred a close study of terrain.'

'Thank you. Take two orbits, Captain Heald, then put us down at G53 T90.'

Heald's plummy repetition was itself echoed in the same vein, though hardly above a whisper, by a voice which could have been Spencer's. Fletcher was beginning to go sour on the role of mentor; but reminded himself that it was, in part, a training mission. He did not single the man out, but said patiently, 'I will remind all personnel that the repetition of executive orders is obligatory and necessary. Confusion on any part of a landfall instruction could turn us into a home-made bomb. Acknowledge.'

Voices came back. Spencer's 'Navigation Three Check,' a shade too prompt. It would do no good there, but it passed the time whilst Heald and Bruce Charlton bombarded communications with raw material for processing.

Finally Heald was ready to move in. He left it later than Dag himself would have done and came out of orbit at a steeper tangent. But it was a workmanlike manœuvre with nothing showy about it. For the final drop, he correctly brought in the robot pilot and the computers put out a string to the selected spot, so that *Interstellar X* could slide down it like a bobbin.

The corvette came down, a plummetting gannet, retro rockets steadied her miles above the pad and she began to sink down through a green twilight. It was a heavy atmosphere. Thermal index was stretching into the red sector. Heald fidgeted. Dag knew what he was thinking. If the heat shields went, they would never lift the ship off again, even if they were still there to do it. On the other hand, blasting off again at this point would not help. There was as far to go out as in. The point of no return had already passed.

Fortunately, in this service there was rarely long to regret. The split second decision was followed in its split second by success or failure, so absolute that reflection was not possible. The gauges had hit emergency and automatically, the last line of defence was brought in. Clouding the direct vision ports, streamers of heavy grey gas were being released from the base to stream back and damp down molecular agitation.

Then they were excavating a private silo in a floor of soft, green soapstone which lay at the bottom of a shaft they had driven through criss crossed limbs of vegetation. Unusual liquid content, as though they had breached pumping lines, was being converted to super-heated steam in boiling clouds; until the heat itself cauterised the severed, writhing ends.

Final stages were so quick that the last scanner pictures before impact were still the best version of what lay above. *Interstellar X* was flexing back in her Chaldean death pit, whilst Fletcher ran the final series through again. Closely observed in slow motion, it became clear that the surface had the texture of smooth muscle. A network of matted, fibrous creeper covered every square centimetre of the ground above. Depth, to be guessed at, as the ship went to earth, could be as much as twenty metres king-sized macaroni.

Dag Fletcher had seen enough to know that his choice of landfall was not going to make him an all time favourite with the geologists. It looked, indeed, as though there would have to be another orbit and a fresh start. But in the meantime, there were enough close pictures to analyse to give them a better chance next time. And in any event they were well screened from any other ship.

There was a curious sense of entombment, although the ship was no darker and the purely visual clues could not have suggested a changed environment. Aurally, there was something fresh, a deadening of sound, as though they were in an acoustic booth. Psychologically the effect was immediate, knowing they were down a hole shrank their narrow world, and made the constraining couches a claustrophobic hell.

Fletcher sensed the impression that was being made and began to fill people's lives with busy care. Cooling was taking longer in the confined space and there was every reason to think that trimming the ship for take-off would be a considerable chore. He got Tamar Kelly and her two assistants preparing a ground map from data so far collected. Dr. Tancred and Vanora were detailed to set up survey teams. Marsh was set to prepare for blast off power-wise, and the navigators were asked to draft a course line for exploratory orbits and another one to get them back to Fingalna.

Vernon Spencer took time off to pause at the communications' console, where Tamar, with visor hinged back, and her hair tight clipped in a white band, was pulling sketch maps together in a fair copy that covered a ten mile square round the ship. He said, 'It looks a load of green tripe to me. Where do you put a Wells Fargo office in that Eldorado?'

'There may be better sites.'

'There'll need to be.' He felt a dig in the centre of his back and found Vanora, sticking out of her shell like a small silver prawn.

She said, 'You will be one of my survey party.'

He turned away with her and they talked quietly, as isolated as if they had been alone on an island.

'But who will be monarch of all he surveys? Or is it to be an oligarchy?'

'I weally never *know* what you mean. Bwadley Heald and Stuart Marsh are with me and Don. With you, that makes five of us. Ask your fwend Tamar to work out two aweas of search.'

'Who's in the other party?'

'Commander Fletcher, Dr. Tancwed, Bwuce Charlton, your fwend Tamar and that nice Iwish boy, Les Wooney.'

'You make it sound very cosy.'

Spencer was no fool and could see that Vanora had managed it very well. She must have got on to Heald straight away. He tried to analyse his own position. How far was he prepared to go along with Vanora? There was, for a start, more to it than she had yet admitted. The lisp, though no doubt genuine, was no mask for the tough character that lay behind it. Not being at all deceived, he had watched her very closely and saw that she was, in reality, immensely self-centred and coldly efficient. It was a combination that pleased him and appealed to some similar characteristics in himself. He had no ties that bothered him. Going over to O.G.A., if it became necessary, was not a step that would matter. What did concern him was whether or not Vanora was quite clever enough. His preferred side was whichever side was going to win.

'Staying in the ship,' Vanora went on, in one of her few boring habits of exploring every situation to its obvious last details, 'There will be only Cormac, Wichard Campbell, Josephine and your other fwend Jacqueline. That should be no pwoblem.'

Again he wondered how far he would have to go and faced the fact that it did not matter. He listened to Vanora and said to himself, 'Spencer, you are a right bastard. Where is your *esprit de corps*? Where is your loyalty to Europe, Earth? Don't you think it matters to be a Galactic Tago?' Frank negative answers came up to this subjective opinion poll. So he said, 'Well, if you don't think it matters, I can't force you. Keep a very close watch on this one, though. I wouldn't like you to get hurt.'

Aloud he said, 'Vanora, your worthy cause has all my immoral support; but if you have a fault, it's a tendency to go on too long. Watch it now, and we'll get along fine.' Then he picked her up and hung her by her harness from an extinguisher rack. It was a good two minutes, before she could get to her intercom and ask to be put down. Strangely enough she did not resent it. She felt that she knew exactly where she was with Spencer. But the look which followed his re-treating back might have made him pause.

Stuart Marsh limped his way to the command console to report in person that it was cool enough to take a look outside.

Dag said, 'Take your people out and see what there is to do. I want us set up for a quick move out. Air samples back straight away. Usual drill.'

He remembered other landfalls, with a corvette at full military readiness, getting out with the skin still hot to secure a bridgehead and stop the local residents from inviting total destruction. All told, they were not too badly off. Probably a message back to I.G.O. at this stage would clear the air. Now that they were in position, it could be claimed, legitimately, that possession had been established by occupation and any move by O.G.A. forces would be direct aggression. They would probably not be prepared to go to those lengths; because such action could only end one way.

He began a definite entry in the sealed log. Tamar could then play it back and send it out as a clear message to I.G.O. She would need the cone antenna up for a land based transmission. Its slender, fifty metre probe would be invisible above ground.

'Day 25 (R.T.) 1549 hours. Landed on Planet Thirza G53 T90 on projection one, filed as appendix to the entry.' He went on to describe the surface and their location. Vanora had supplied him with details of her survey setup and he included that. Marsh called in with a preliminary statement on atmospheric conditions; so he went on, 'Breathable air. Slightly oxygen rich. Detailed analysis proceeding.' He ended with a text book bit from the I.G.O. charter, relevant to the situation of first physical landing on planets in an agreed sphere of influence. 'Commissar Cormac is now regarded as I.G.O. Consul and *Interstellar X* has diplomatic neutrality as I.G.O. headquarters in this place.'

When it was done he passed a copy over to Tamar Kelly. 'As soon as you like. Push this out to I.G.O. In clear. Now that we're here it might as well be known to all and some what the score is. In any case an interested party would soon crack the standard codes.'

'Arrival entry to I.G.O. in clear. Check.'

She shifted the material which was filling the presentation table of her console, methodically returning charts sheets to deep vertical files. When she was ready, she carefully assessed outgoing signal strength and put in another bit of chat to the headman. 'I confirm that external aerial extension is necessary. Permission to put out extensor.'

He was expecting it, and had been looking at the scene above. It was a fish's view of a circle of green sky. There seemed no reason to suppose that the probe would poke itself into any trouble. 'Go ahead.'

The scanner itself gave them a close picture of the cone, and they saw the delicate-looking probe begin to extrude like a spontaneously forming plastic rod. At ten metres, with the tip almost clear of the walls of their well, it appeared to shatter like a dropped glass. Fractionally later, there was the thud of an explosion from inside the ship and a pressure wave that slapped into their ears.

The action stations call was sounding before the noise had died away. Marsh came on urgently from outside, where he and his two assistants were still working with trimming jacks to prepare for take-off. 'Hold that extensor. It's breaking up.' It was an automatic warning, he did not stop to ask himself whether or not it was a party matter.

Spencer, on his way to the navigation console, made a detour to cut off Vanora on her way to her isolated station. He gave her platinum silk head a congratulatory pat. 'Clever.'

'I don't know what you mean.'

'Don't give me that. Remember you're talking to Uncle Vernon.'

She looked genuinely puzzled. So much so, that he said, 'Me, remember, blood brothers.'

They were angled so that his bulky figure screened her

from what was going on elsewhere. He wedged her firmly against the bulkhead and thoughtfully selected one of the longer cords from the ravel that dangled down her chest. Before she could understand what he was about, he had slipped it into the open rim of her visor and across her throat. Then he began to pull it tight as though carrying out some kind of impersonal experiment. Her head was forced back, but the green eyes held his without any fear.

She appeared to come to a decision about him. 'It was set a long time ago. Just a tiny one. It detonates by signal.'

'Any others about?'

He pulled in another centimetre of cord. It was doubtful whether she would be able to answer at all; but in the event, she was saved the bother. Bruce Charlton was getting impatient. He had not yet been able to clear his section as physically present at the treadmill. He called across, 'Spencer, your love life will have to wait. Report in. Get sealed up. Now, man.'

Spencer had half turned to listen to what was being said and with surprising strength, Vanora pushed herself away from the wall and ducked clear. The good moment for an exchange of confidences had gone. Still, he was quite satisfied. He seemed to be with the more vigorous party and that was the way he wanted it to be. But he was under no illusions about Vanora. He would watch that one very carefully indeed.

Dag Fletcher had already handed over to Heald. 'Be ready, Captain, to take us out. Get Marsh in as soon as he's finished. Communications One and Two with me. I want to know what we have to put right.'

Tamar gave the keys of her kingdom to Les Rooney. 'Don't try any crystal ball stuff, Paddy, just go by the book. We'll be right back.' Then she was shuffling out through the hatch, clumsy in the heavy suit at full gravity.

Vertically at rest, the ship was unfamiliar. Moving about was now a straight climb up or down steep companions and cutaway footholds. The final circular hatch, above the hydroponic tank section was grotesquely twisted back as if tweaked open by a giant thumb. Above it the cone narrowed sharply and there was only room to crouch. In the centre of the space, like a tent pole, was the tubular housing of the flexible extensor probe, ripped jaggedly down its whole length and spilling its mechanisms on to the deck. It was a write-off.

Dag plugged himself in on Tamar's intercom, using the single line which kept their chat off the general net.

'Any ideas about this?'

'If you mean *who* did it or *why*, not a thing. If you mean, *how*, I suppose something detonated on a signal. Only an expert could piece it together though.'

'Can you do anything with it?'

'Not unless we carry a complete spare.'

'We don't.'

'Nothing then. But it doesn't matter a great deal. If the hull is sound, the communications difficulty can be got over. We only use this on the ground. I can rig a land aerial which will work just as well. In flight we won't be affected.'

'How long?'

'Depends what it's like up top. A few hours. One of the engineers and Dick here will be all the personnel I need.'

'Good. I leave it to you then. Brief Campbell now and get on with it. I want to check the skin over this place. You've no thoughts, then, about who might do this?'

'I certainly don't trust Vanora; but there's no reason to suppose she would want to wreck the ship.'

'It could well be to stop our communication with I.G.O. so get on with your alternative.'

'Check.'

Fletcher swung himself through the hatch and dropped heavily to the next bulkhead. He was beginning to feel very angry with the whole pointless business. What had begun as a commercial and training flight had gathered such complications to itself that the mission was drifting towards a first class muddle. The planet looked bad enough. They were awkwardly placed in their cramping silo. Land survey was going to be no picnic at all. He had to find a site and leave it equipped as the local consulate. And someone inside the ship was working against him. That too, made very little sense; because surely no one would suppose that the I.G.O. Central office would give up after a few setbacks? Next time it would be a squadron and overwhelming strength.

By this time, he was in the lock. He raised Heald on the intercom. 'Commander to Captain. No continuing danger. Stand down, but be ready for a quick recall. Get a survey party ready to go out. It had better be Vanora's. Let her indicate an area of search and take out the loading trolley, that should cope with this terrain all right.'

Even through the correct, plummy delivery, Heald sounded pleased with the idea. Perhaps he was a Vanora fan. Fletcher was out and climbing again in a green tinged gloom up the silver grey side of the towering ship. The exit lock was about central and he could see only vague movement thirty metres below, where Marsh and his trogs were still working with the trimming jacks.

Interstellar X had made itself a funnel-shaped excavation; climbing slowly, he passed the true ground level and looked, without stopping, at the vegetation. It appeared to have no rooting system, but lay like close packed strands of rope. Movement would be on its living surface and a lot would depend on how firm that was.

Then he was concentrating on the ship. A white precipitate was coating the top ten metres. He brushed with his gauntlet and found that it came away like dust. Something, no doubt, left by the evaporating liquid from the *lianas*. He collected enough for a sample and put it in a belt pouch.

The first good news of the day came when he hauled himself conscientiously over the tip of the steeple and found that it was intact. Seemingly, the blast had been all down. The only thing to do was to get on with the programme and get out. If Vanora had anything to do with the sabotage, she was

better out on a survey job than in. Once the report to I.G.O.
had been made, there was very little any agent could do to
reverse the machinery of law.

When he climbed back into his ship, he found the survey
party ready to go. Never one to worry about the command
image, he changed his mind about using the power trolley.

'Take the scout car, Captain. That will save time. Clearly,
we can't stay here. What daylight have we got?'

'Nightfall 1830 hours ship time.'

'That gives you two hours for a preliminary look round.
See what you can find as a more permanent pad. Something
that might be developed into a small space port.'

'Check.'

Vanora looked very pleased at the change. It would be more
comfortable and increase their range. She went with Marsh,
who had reported in from below, to the small compartment
which housed the multipurpose excursion module. He raised
the outer wall and dim green light filtered into the tiny space.
Then the four-seater scout car was sidling out into the funnel.

At the main lock he left it hovering with Vanora on board,
whilst he rounded up the rest of their party. When they
finally got away, with Don Voller crouched in the loading
bay surrounded by emergency stores and Vanora's survey
gear, they had one and three quarter hours left to the deadline of nightfall.

It was time which quickly passed, substantiating once more
the reasonable theory that a filled interval is subjectively
shorter than one spent contemplating one's navel. Tamar,
having climbed laboriously with her equipment to the surface found it impracticable to set up an aerial system. Under-
foot the loose rubbery trailing ropes shifted and sank. It was
almost impossible to stay upright and totally impossible to
secure guy lines to portable telescopic masts.

She reported back and got a laconic. 'Back inside. I'll clear
a space.'

When they were out of the way, he swivelled the corvette's main armament and sent a searing blast at ground level. For a kilometre, on a fifty metre front, the vegetation ceased to exist. The green stone was bare to the sky. Less than thirty minutes later, Tamar had the aerial set up and was making a test transmission from her own console back in the ship.

Dag Fletcher was standing beside her and saw the first look of simple surprise turn to something like dismay.

'What is it?'

'I'm sorry, Dag. I honestly thought this would do it. But there must be a very heavy ionised layer. Nothing we can mount here would punch a signal through it. You can only get in touch with I.G.O. from an orbit. I'm sorry.'

'No need to be. No executive could do more. It doesn't change much. We'll go up as soon as we can establish a place for the consulate. Could you have done it with the antenna?'

'No.'

'So in this case sabotage paid no dividends?'

'Right. And I'd add to that. Nobody else can get a signal out either unless there's some equipment I've never heard of.'

He remembered the sample of powder from the outer skin. 'Since there's no further communications job, run the standard tests on a sample for me.'

In the absence of the five surveyors, a new atmosphere seemed evident in the ship. Dag could not identify it, but it was real enough, and he realised that there had been a continuous sense of strain on this trip, as though he had been working all the time to keep disparate elements in some kind of harmony.

At 1830 hours, green gloom thickened into viridian and then quickly to black night. The tender had not appeared nor did it signal in any fresh notice of intention. When Tamar ran into the day cabin with something like the old friendly intimacy, it was coming up to 2200 hours.

'Dag.'

'Here, present.'
'Do you know what?'
'Not until you tell me.'
'That sample. Do you know what it is?'
'Tell me.'
'It's pure platinum.'

CHAPTER FOUR

WORKING without the antenna, Tamar Kelly could only get a kilometre diameter scan round the ship in its gopher hole. That brought no joy in respect of the time-expired survey party. But, feeling like Dag that their absence did something for the common weal, she could not honestly say that she minded very much. The car was equipped with survival gear which could beat a more hostile environment than this. There was no need to bother about them.

But the communications situation was unique in her experience. It was as though a force was meeting and pushing back her signals. Even full power, enough to light a small city, did not extend their radar horizon. She reported to Dag Fletcher, 'One thing's for sure, Dag, there will be no communication in or out of here by any system on any fleet we know about.'

'Why do you say that?' He had not confided his knowledge of the following frigate or indeed of the developing situation, as he saw it, with O.G.A.

'You remember checking that equipment in Vanora's cabin?'

'Yes. A theodolite.'

'Heavily powered for the job it had to do. I had a closer look at it. It could be coincidence; but the stand looked as though it could do double duty as a dipole.'

They were in the command cabin with Bruce Charlton and his helpmeet, Jacqueline Ann, who was beginning to appreciate the easy good nature of the quiet navigator. It was certainly easier to live with than Vernon Spencer's saturnine and unpredictable charm. Indeed, even she found his absence a relief. It seemed to free her from a kind of pressure, which she could not have avoided, voluntarily.

'Are you sure of that?'

'Not sure; but it could be.'

'Has she taken it on this trip?'

'Yes; but then she would. It *is* a theodolite, whatever else it might be.'

'Is there much left?'

'More than enough.'

'I want you to take Jacqueline with you and check through every item.'

'Now?'

'Very now.'

It was 2138 hours ship's time. He had no expectation that the search party would return until morning. They would set up a survival dome and sleep out. No hardship as far as could be judged. When the two searchers had gone he said, 'What do you make of it, Bruce? Why haven't they come in?'

Bruce Charlton in white Tee shirt, khaki drill pants and sneakers shrugged broad shoulders and began sensitive manipulation of the complex navigation console with huge freckled hands. Sandy hair in an aggressive crew-cut, blue eyes surrounded by a network of small wrinkles, he looked more like a trainee than his sophisticated partner; but it was a misleading appearance. He said, 'Equipment fault might hold them or there could be something over the hill or they simply decided to stay away.'

'Vanora decided?'

'Could be. Can I speak off the record? I don't have any personal axe to grind in this.'

'Tell me.'

'Honestly, I don't like knocking a fellow executive and a senior one at that; but Bradley Heald is peculiar in some of his views. He missed out on I.G.O. service you know. Some mystery about that too; but I do know he has no time for the organisation at all. I believe he might renege if the inducement was high enough. Then Stu. Marsh is very bitter about the service. He would go a long way to square up what he thinks of as an old score. Add to them that king-sized layabout Voller and that awkward sod Spencer and you can see that the girl has gathered together a pretty ripe assortment of box fruit.'

'Thank you very much. Don't worry, you haven't told me anything I didn't know; but it confirms my own views.'

'Why did you let them go out?'

'Until some definite move is made there is no action I can take.'

'Give them enough rope?'

'Something like that. After all, they can do less damage out there than inside.'

'The antenna was sabotage then?'

'Not a doubt.'

'Doesn't that constitute a "definite move"?'

'Yes, but I like to think it has passed off as "undefined causes". I want to know what is intended.'

'I can see that, but the next one could ground us for good.'

There was more truth in that than Dag liked to accept. He was not only risking himself in the way he was playing this thing. Facing that fact, his reply was delayed and then indefinitely postponed as the searchers reappeared at the hatch.

Tamar, first through, and looking pleased, said, 'There's at least one other piece which could be dual purpose. It's a very elaborate sonar device for identifying substrata, but I think it converts into a pretty good laser. And this explained the demolition job.' She held out a small flat case of figured electrum.

Dag carried it to the display table of his console and opened it under the hooded inspection lamp. It was about eight centimetres square and a centimetre deep, a beautiful piece of workmanship; just the sort of thing Vanora would have for cosmetics. He was hardly surprised at all to find inside, ten small cylinders of the same metal each with a flat inset showing a colour sample. A tone card for a range of pale greens. Tweezers and manicure aids took up a centre slot.

'Lipsticks?'

'Yes, but look,' Tamar selected one and gave its milled rim a half turn. A small tongue of colour protruded from the open end. The lipstick was worn evenly, a regular meticulous cone, which in itself was a revealing gloss on the character of their absent friend. Self-centred, unfettered by burdensome loyalties. Tamar suddenly realised that her own use of that item left a diagonal slant on the material. Did that tell any tales about her character? She gave it a further twist and the bottom half centimetre came away altogether and she tipped out a small solid-looking black disc. 'That's the bomb.'

'How detonated?'

'Voice signal possible or low power transmission. But it could be set for a simple gravity hold and release at an altitude. Could use a modification on the intercom. It's a neat job.'

'How many are there?'

'Six left.'

'That means or could mean that four have been placed. One we know about. Three others then. Can you fix these so that they would not respond to signal?'

'Yes, I think so.'

'Tell me how and I'll do that, then we can look for the rest.'

'It will be safer if I do it.'

'Not safer for you.'

It was mildly said, but with a finality that brooked no argument. She only hesitated fractionally, then went on, 'The base comes off and there's a setting needle, for frequency, but she might check that. There must be a way of disarming it. Try withdrawing the whole face. With the tweezers.'

He was working as she spoke and had the tiny front piece slowly coming off. Beneath it was a micro mechanism which was no doubt the receiver, and a tiny solid compartment.

'The spindle from the pointer goes into that centre barrel. Must engage there and turn the whole thing.'

Tamar's head was now between him and the device. He gently pushed it away. 'Right. I see it all. Go and look for the three missing thimbles, I'll join you when this is done.'

'Where shall we look?'

'Think where Vanora could get.'

'Almost anywhere I'd say.' It was the first flaw in the newly woven mat of peace and she quickly went on, 'But she would want to be in a position to neutralise power or navigation, or perhaps communications again.'

'Off you go then and work at it. Go on. Move.'

Reluctantly she backed out through the hatch, watching him to the last. Charlton and Jacqueline Ann were already down in the narrow confines of the power pack. Ten minutes later they had their first success. It was just inside the service panel of the subsidiary control console; if it had blown when Power Two was sitting at her lonely action station, she would have taken the blast down the centre of her chest.

'It was there all the time I was sitting there.'

Charlton put a massive arm round her shoulders, 'Don't think too much about that, Jacky. When you think about the hazards of any straightforwad trip, it's only adding a fraction to the risk. Statistically negligible.'

'That's a big comfort. But thanks a lot. I know you mean well.'

Tamar had already withdrawn the cap and was looking at the needle setting. It meant nothing until it was related to some instruction key. She carefully noted the position and then rotated the needle to the safe zero position as on the ones not yet set. Then she pulled out the face which disengaged the spindle from the barrel. Tweezers from her own belt pouch served to snap off the thin stalk, after which she reassembled it and reset the pointer.

'Now it looks the same, but nothing is set inside.'

'You're sure of that? I should hate you to be wrong.'

'If I'm wrong you won't be in a position to hate anybody.'

'Tamar isn't wrong, you can rely on that.' Bruce Charlton gave the colourful cadet a reassuring pat where evolution had clearly intended it should fall, and earned himself a more friendly smile than any yet.

Over an hour of search went on before they had another success. In the interim, the unused bombs had been made safe and the case returned to its usual place. Dag narrowed the search to the control room. 'I believe the other two must be somewhere in here. She would hardly waste them on structural damage. Power, she fixed down below. Communications again is likely. One there and one in the navigation console is my guess.'

The one in the communications slot was slipped at about shoulder level in a small gap between two piano key switches. It would have wrecked the console and taken Tamar's right arm off.

'Have you been bullying your little room mate?'

'Wait until the last one turns up, Bruce, then we'll see who was her favourite.'

But, in the event, it did not turn up. At 2300 hours, Dag said, 'Leave it at that. It isn't likely to be detonated just yet. There would be nothing to gain. We'll keep an eye open for it, if it isn't found before take off I'll just have to wring it out of Vanora.'

'She'll enjoy that.' Tamar could not help saying it and was immediately annoyed with herself.

Les Rooney coming in to take his share of the anchor watch created a diversion. He had been looking out through the direct vision ports and seemed to find something unusual about the half power picture which was currently released on the scanner. His cabin was well up towards the cone and faced the cleared area, so that he had a view over the lip of their burrow on to the open ground.

'Commander.'

'What is it, Rooney?'

'This picture. The cutting there is just an empty piece of bare ground.'

'That's right. You saw it that way in daylight.'

'It doesn't look like that from the direct vision port.'

'How does it look from there?'

'Filled in. Not with vegetation though. That's why I came straight to the scanner to take a look. Filled in with buildings.'

Tamar said, 'It's the Little People been at it again.'

Dag Fletcher had been in strange places often enough to know that any imaginable thing was possible. 'I'll take a look.' He and Tamar went up to the gunnery centre, higher than Voller's cabin, between one section of hydroponic tanks and the cone. It faced the clearing, vertically above the other, indeed Dag had used its direct fire controls to do the instant deforestation. He activated the turret screens and the inner wall began to slice itself back in parabolic segments. Now they had a grandstand view of the narrow canyon and a dark smudge of distant horizon where darkness thickened to solid black and the pale green starlight shaded out.

Tamar said uncertainly, 'I know that place. It's a farm. Yes, it's getting clearer all the time. It's a replica of where I was brought up. Cheshire, England. But there should be a water tower on a pylon, way back against a rising slope with a copse on top.' Her voice left its husky depths in a sudden crack of excitement. 'And there it is. I can see it now.'

'Near the fly-over?'

'You must be joking.'

'No,' his voice was very serious. 'I see the central square of an underground city I once came across. There's a piazza. Mosaic work.'

'You can never see the floor!'

'Clearly. I nearly died on it. There's a picture of a dark

girl. A market scene. Laughing. Skin of pale copper. White teeth. Oval face, eyes of a Hindu dancing girl. Transparent blouse with a belt of elliptical gold links. Heavily pleated red skirt. Sandals laced high.'

Tamar had abandoned her farm with a great effort of will, as the hallucinatory effect seemed to be strengthening all the time and was watching his face with a hand on his arm as he leaned against the rim of the port. 'Dag, you were in love with her. Who was she?'

'I don't know.'

He turned away and met her eyes. She could see he was deeply moved.

'Tell me about her.'

'It was on Plantos Three, all of twenty years ago. I was commanding an I.G.O. corvette like this one. *Petrel*. Part of a squadron, mopping up after that Fingalnian break away. We finally cornered the last of their super ships, hidden in an abandoned city on a dead world. I don't know who she was, but I saw her picture twice. Once on a mural and once on the mosaic. For years she was more real to me than any living person. She made me move when I was only half conscious and would have died if I hadn't.'

Tamar said with sudden insight. 'She's the most dangerous rival a girl could have. You'll never believe that she would only be the same as the rest of us. She won't age and she will never misunderstand.'

'I can recognise illusion, even my own.'

He looked at the vivid, golden eyed girl beside him. 'You don't have to worry about competition, living or dead.'

Cormac, the Venusian, had toiled heavily up the nearly vertical companions to join them. He said, 'I believe there is some mystery, Commander. A discrepancy between the mechanical eye and the fallible biological one. May I see?'

He took a long look and Dag moved back to the opposite bulkhead, where he leaned with an arm round Tamar's waist. She put her head on his shoulder and a soft cushion of silky hair pressed the side of his face. What she had said had enough truth in it to bring him up face to face with the subjective realities. It was a sonar beam, probing the underwater mass of the iceberg psyche, needling down in that hidden country, where each man is a stranger in his own mind.

Cormac said heavily, 'I see the landscape of Venus and a place which I know well. I see what it is, Commander, this is an effect which has been observed, very occasionally, before. Each one will see something which is very near to his heart. Something which is always vividly present in the sub-conscious, a nearly permanent pattern of certain mental bonds. These bonds are so strong that they have resisted the disintegrating effect of whatever force this is. Ordinary associ-ation of ideas is inhibited. It is as though the scene were given a kind of shadow life there.'

'To what good end?'

'Let us hope to some good end, in fact, Lieutenant Kelly; because an organism of such power has us in the hollow of its hand. Should it use its power to destroy our minds instead of merely to observe them, we have no defence.'

Dag said, 'Not quite, Commissar. I agree with what you say, but the power must be directional. Only these ports are affected. However refined it is, it must be a form of energy. It can probably go wherever light can go. The skin of the ship might well be an adequate screen.'

'Yes, yes. You could be right, of course. It raises doubts about the safety of the survey party. Also problems about our stay here.' Cormac moved away from the port before he con-tinued, and stood squatly facing them, with his heavy, square shoulders against a solid bulkhead. 'You see, Commander, you will have to neutralise this force, before we can get on with our mission. And I must warn everyone to think only the most friendly thoughts when they are in direct line of an outer port. We don't want any antagonism to be suspected, until we are in a position where we need not fear reprisals.'

'That's sound reasoning.'

'I have often needed to secure my personal safety before saying unwelcome things. The long term good is not always self evident.'

Tamar had a convulsive grip on Dag's arm. Cormac had a habit of following her about with his eyes which she sometimes found unnerving; this was the first sustained conversation she had taken part in with him and it improved his image. Instead of giving her the creeps his solemn, assumption that his 'personal safety' would be as important to them as to himself made her want to giggle. But she kept up her end of the chat by taking the professional communications angle. 'Beamed energy must have a source. It will be identifiable as a frequency. I might be able to isolate it and then do a cross-scanning job to pin-point the place of origin.'

Cormac said with old world courtesy, 'It is unusual to find anyone so beautiful who is also so clever. I think you should do that right away.'

Dag said, 'I agree, we should do that; but seeing our private worlds is not going to do any harm for a few hours. Start at first light. It can be part of the survey chore. The crunch will come if there is any attempt to influence our minds.'

Cormac said, 'With all respect, Commander, knowledge of such an attempt may well come too late, or, indeed, not at all, if the move has been successfully made. I suggest that any party working in the open should be screened.'

Fletcher was never one to reject good advice. 'Of course, you are quite right, Commissar. We will look into the whole question in the morning. One thing for now, Tamar, get on to the duty executive and have the power screen switched in.'

'That's me, I'm afraid; but Rooney will be able to do it.'

She was already at the console and speaking to him. His leprechaun's face came up on the small screen. 'Your little people are still at it, Les. Bring in the power screen, starting low; and keep this link open. Tell me about it as you go.'

He worked at it, only momentarily leaving the picture.
'Coming in now. Zero reading. Taking it to half a point.'

'Hold it there.'

Dag was looking out again. He signalled for more power
and she relayed like a peon in a bucket chain.

Dag said, 'We're meeting it there. Just a little more. Right.
Hold it at that. Take a look, Commissar.'

Cormac said, 'So. That's very good as far as it goes. There
is nothing there for me now. You have swamped any incoming signal. Or distorted it. It could happen that way.'

'I'll settle for the first. Now we should get some rest. Tomorrow could be a busy day.' Dag's voice had a flat finality
in it. He knew now he had to think in terms of a campaign
and for that you needed to husband your resources.

The pale green light of Thirza moved evenly to full strength,
as if on a rheostat. Twilight and dawn were only rudimentary
in this equatorial zone. Dag saw the light come up from the
gunnery capsule where he had spent the night in the gunner's
swivel couch. Bare green stone floored the cutting. He prodded
a call button and got Freya Burleigh's calm face filling the
screen.

He said, 'What does the power screen stand at?'

'No change. Mark 2.'

'Thank you, Freya. Pull the plug will you. There's work to
do and we need an early start. Couple it with a verbal instruction to report in shore kit.'

Bleeps began to sound through the ship. In their rocky silo
they had a deeper note and some of the urgency had gone
out of the alarm. Freya Burleigh's well modulated voice made
the reporting instructions sound like an invitation to a garden
party. Not everyone was aware of the new development, so
Dag gave a general briefing.

He ended with, 'So we have to try it out by easy stages.
The power trolley can put up a fair screen, which will be
strong enough to match the force as of now. How much

further it might have to go, of course, can't be guessed at. In the first instance, I want Executive Kelly, Freya Burleigh and Dick Campbell out with me and we'll do a trial circuit, aiming to be back by noon. With restricted communications we shall have to make short reconnaissance runs and return to base each time. Should we not return Executive Charlton is in command and I advise you, Bruce, now, to blast off and take a parking orbit over this place. From there you can talk to I.G.O. and get instructions.'

Quarter of an hour later, they were moving along the cleared bed of green rock, all four standing on the loading bay of a small caterpillar-tracked trolley. It had been tricky getting it ashore from the cargo elevator between *Interstellar X's* lofty tripod legs. Finally it had been winched across the gap to the clearing, to securing holds cut out of the living rock by Campbell. When they reached him, he was completely confused. He had gone on, doggedly following the last instruction he had been given; but he believed he was surrounded by masonry. He had excavated his niches in what appeared to be the wall of his own home. Only his hands had told him that it was rock.

Once on the narrow platform, they were within a bell-shaped screen of energy put up by the powerful motors of the trolley and the landscape resumed its normal appearance. Or as Freya Burleigh said, with unusual penetration, 'Normal as far as we know. It may bear no relation at all to what is really there.'

At the end of the valley, there was a tangle of green tubular vegetation angled in its run across their front. The motor sank its quiet hum a semitone and took them up without a check. At one point, the strands had packed themselves into a one in one gradient and they were hanging on to the tubular half hoops which served as sides.

Tamar said, 'It's slow; but more sure than the hover car. Now, I realise, they would be sitting ducks for grand scale illusion. It has no all-round energy screen.'

'It has a circular, forward facing screen.' Dag was only partly listening and was feeding more power to the left track to take them out of an impossible overhang. 'Yes, but who knows which is the key direction in this case?'

'All right, I take the point. Once we're on top you can start. What are you going to use?'

'This energy screen virtually puts up a jamming barrage over a whole frequency band. I can cut frequencies out systematically until we find which one it is that cancels the incoming force. Then I can get a binaural directional fix on that one frequency. Next stop we try again and we have it nailed on two lines.'

'X marks the spot.'

'I don't see why not.'

They ground their way over the yielding rubbery lip of the incline and a long undulating vista, of very nearly damn all, stretched away to every horizon.

Freya Burleigh looked at it without any enthusiasm. 'They say Venus is a landscape painter's Golgotha; but it can't have anything on this. It'll make Cormac believe he came from Paradise.'

Fletcher notched up the speed and they trundled on in a roller coaster ride. He coaxed it along to over a kilometre a minute and much of the minor vibration was ironed out as they skimmed the tops of the close packed strands. After ten minutes, with the horizon virtually unchanged, he slowed to a stop. 'Try it then, Tamar.'

She had already worked out a time-saving sequence on a random sample basis and was busy within seconds of the stop, with the inspection panel of the motor stripped away and a pair of leads tapping its screen building circuits.

The rest sat outside the trolley just within the narrow hemisphere of its protecting shell of force. Campbell was first to see it go. In the act of lighting a cigarette, he let it fall from his opening mouth to say excitedly, 'There it is again. My house. Yorkshire stone. And the name, by God, on the gate, GREY STONES. How original can you get?'

Tamar, whose reflexes were faster than most had locked on to the frequency before confirmation came from anywhere else. But it came quickly and she glanced up herself to check that her own farm was amongst those present. It was.

'That's it then, Dag. I've got the frequency. Now I want to put out two dish aerials and get a fix on it.'

'Do that. Give us the full screen back.'

Richard Campbell picked his way deliberately over the bare green surface. The other three watched him miming his way through a gate and following a path towards his private house. He put the aerial he was carrying on the centre of its lawn and looked very pleased about it. He came back towards them with the second dish.

Freya, startled out of her customary calm, said, 'He's leaving it in mid air.'

The scene had obviously dominated Campbell. He was not looking towards them. He had placed the second aerial on a flat coping stone on the garden wall and was waiting for the next thing. They saw him sit down and then stretch out as though he was lying on a grassy bank.

Dag said, 'As quick as you can, Tamar. He's heavily hypnotised. There'll be no progress on this planet until we sort this out.'

She needed no urging. In fifteen seconds of delicate tuning she had established a compass direction and recorded it. 'You can get him in.'

Dag Fletcher hitched a light line to a belt toggle and went out through the screen. He was immediately on the tiled floor of the spacious piazza of his underground city. Only blind determination drove him forward in the direction he had set. They saw him fall to his hands and knees and crawl on. When he stopped, just short of Campbell, Tamar knew he was looking again at his dark, pale skinned girl. She was willing him to go on, but when he did, she could not believe that any influence of hers had moved him. Then he was brushing blindly into the man on the grass and they saw him grip Campbell's wrists. Tamar began to haul in on the line, using the winch. Fletcher was compelled to come in and he brought the other man with him.

Freya Burleigh volunteered to bring back the equipment and she managed very well. Her private world was a sloping lawn in a provincial park. She was walking across it to a far corner, where black trees with huge, bare, dark branches made a grid of lines against the sky and she knew that, as on a morning years ago, he would not be there. It was worse than the time itself; because even the pleasure of anticipation was coloured by this retroactive despair; that she was really alone was now part of the mental furniture. Then it had been still to learn.

She was guided by Tamar; a kind of double think, answered signals on the cord which seemed hardly relevant to the situation she appeared to be in. When she was back inside the screen she was paler than usual and quite silent.

Dag went off at a ninety degree angle to the line roughed in by Tamar and after ten minutes they tried again. This time it was working to a system and Dag found that by absolute concentration on the signals he was able to discount the image. Given enough time, he believed he might beat it altogether; though it was like hacking at his mind with a blunt saw to attempt it.

Working quickly on the floor of the trolley, Tamar had a sketch map with compass directions minutes after the last reading had been taken. She said, 'Well, there it is. Almost due north of the ship. North North East by North at 350 to 400 kilometres, I should say. That's the source.'

'Thank you. That was very well done. We'll make a detour and get back to the ship, then set out again directly on that course.'

Mile after mile, in a sweeping circle, sometimes running directly with the line of the pipe-like fibres, the trolley hit its most efficient speed at a steady mile a minute. When the scenery changed, it was so sudden that Dag stopped within feet of the edge of a basin-shaped depression, where the lianas had diverged left and right to leave bare rock and a deep clear eye of water.

It was unusual enough to merit a closer look and he took the trolley down to the green shore, a narrow shelf of smooth rock. It was like finding a private swimming pool in the middle of the Sahara. Dag edged the trolley to the brink and they looked down into clear translucent water with a slight surface shimmer which made a litter of stone shapes on the bottom expand and contract by refraction. He moved slowly along the bank.

Campbell said suddenly, 'There's Vanora.' A pale white figure between two pinnacles of green rock was clearly human, and, once the recognition had been made, was likely to be Vanora.

Dag was already hooking himself to the line. He was through the screen and diving into the stone floor of his private piazza before anyone else had moved.

Underwater, he was in the real world again, insulated from the intrusive frequency by the thick blanket of liquid over him. It was denser than sea water and it was a fight against buoyancy to take himself down the eight metres to where the white figure lay. Then he had it round the waist under one arm and was shooting up into illusion.

Tamar brought him in like a monstrous fish and they saw him stand on the shelving beach and wade out with a life-size replica of Vanora in what appeared to be white crystal. He put it down and it stood leaning against him. Vanora in very truth, in perfection of physical proportion, standing with hands to her sides and right foot slightly advanced like a figure stepping out of a marble bas relief.

The line tightened again and he was led forward towards them. He picked up his model and carried her in front of him, presenting her back to the viewers, a delight in itself to any *aficionado* of the classic form, though viewed with something less than charity by Tamar. She could not help thinking that it was just like Vanora to be found in scene-stealing nudity even as a fossil.

Dag came up the slope like a marionette and walked straight into the screen. As the white figure entered its disruptive field, there was a flicker as though a flame had been blown out and Dag appeared at the side of the trolley with empty hands.

Observation is the basis of true science; but some detail is best promulgated in the written record. He said, 'Curiously enough, it was not a perfect replica. Vanora had a small, black, anvil-shaped mark just left of centre below the navel, and the model did not.'

Tamar gave him a look which would be scripted in a silent melodrama of the early technological age as 'a slow burn'. She said, 'Naturally, *anybody* would notice that.'

At the ship, they signalled for a line and went out, one at a time, through their private worlds to the solid screen of the corvette. Tamar would neither speak to him nor allow him to explain, and he realised that he would have to look for a better time. There was, anyway, only one good way of making it clear and that might have to wait.

Bruce Charlton met him at the main entry port, 'This screen, Dag. We've had to take it up. We're running it at Mark3. There's been a gradual rise all morning. What happens when we can't meet it?'

CHAPTER FIVE

DAG FLETCHER was rapidly tiring of being at the receiving end of other people's initiative. The resurrection of the scene on Plantos Three carried with it some overtone of his personality at that time and he knew that the years had changed him a lot. At that time, he would have taken *Petrel* up on a positive counter move. Now he was the conservative, senior man, moving slowly, waiting for an opponent's move. Even telling himself that it was a far cry from a fully manned military unit to the armed merchantman he now had was no sufficient comfort.

He went into the command cabin with Charlton and expounded his appreciation of the situation they were in. Tempting though it might be, to blast off and sort it out from overhead, there were at least two good reasons for staying put and sweating it out at ground level. For one, Vanora might still be able to detonate her last bomb if she saw the corvette begin to move. More important, there was no way of knowing what had happened to the following frigate. It could well be in a parking orbit itself and ready to convert them to molecular trash.

Dag said, 'We'll take a spell for an hour, then we'll have another look for the survey party. We have a line now on the source of this mind bender. Within four hundred kilometres. Say six hours. We'll take a closer look and get back sometime tomorrow.'

'Same group?'

'I'd like to take Cormac, he's a very knowledgeable man.

Leave out Freya. You might need a navigator. If you have to go up, you'll be hard pressed for staff.'

'No chance of me coming along?'

'I'd like to have you there, Bruce, but it just isn't on. There's got to be one executive here.'

'Check.'

He felt more satisfied now that he had a positive line to follow. His mind turned to the personal problem of making peace with Tamar. She must have known that he would have gone carefully through the very detailed physical records of the personnel files. After all, in some circumstances, identification could be a dodgy issue and matters like unusual skin markings were always noted. He rightly estimated that she was more piqued by his self-confessed private illusion than by the comment on Vanora's anvil.

Her cabin was empty; but she had changed, because pants and sweater, worn on the morning chore, were thrown across the acceleration couch. Splashes of white and vivid, electric blue. There was something rather pathetic and defenceless about the empty clothing. In the context of this remote corner of galactic space, it made a kind of forlorn human gesture, as indeed did a residual fragrance of her scent with its characteristic harmonic of sandalwood.

The wardroom contained Jacqueline Ann, Les Rooney and Cormac, watching gravely like an ethnologist putting in some case study. In the absence of her evil genius, the girl was rapidly turning into a minor life and soul, which in this instance was leading her to demonstrate an Irish Jig to a jaunty electronic fiddle and a frenetic clap of the off beat by the bhoy himself.

With womanly intuition, she guessed that Dag was looking for Tamar Kelly and without stopping she jigged over to the door and said, 'Ye'll foind the young leddy in the attic.'

Tamar was looking out of the direct vision port on to her Cheshire farm and when he came quietly behind her, she did not move. Without going into the line of the beam himself, he stretched out to take her shoulders in a firm grip and pulled her away. When he turned her to face him, her eyes were wide open with enormous black pupils and shiny with unshed tears.

He backed himself against the protective bulkhead and slowly bent his arms, so that she was forced to move her feet and shuffle reluctantly towards him. Some of the mesmerised look was wearing off and as her pupils contracted slightly, her eyes regained their golden brown warmth.

Her arms were by her sides and she made no move, until the slow flexing brought the tips of her breasts against the hard line of his lower ribs. There he stopped and took his hands from their grip. They stood still and silent with only the soft, pneumatic contact changing pressure with their quiet breathing. Through the thin fabrics, he could feel a growing firmness, a tautening, which was involuntary on her part. Her eyes told him that she knew it, and knew that he did; but would stubbornly make no move.

His hands went slowly under the thick bell of silky hair and long, strong fingers cupped the shape of her head and then her arms were round his neck, pulling his face down to her own.

Explanation, at this level, was out of place and he was wise enough to know it, With her arms still round his neck, he lifted her off her feet and carried her over to the acceleration couch.

'Do you really love me?'

'You know it.'

'More than that grinning, dark girl on the pavement?'

'I don't even know her name; but after all she did save my life. It would be inhuman not to be grateful.'

'That's not what I asked.'

She was struggling to sit up, and he knew he had said the wrong thing. Why couldn't he have told a quick, diplomatic lie? But somehow, he could not be false to that image, which the intrusive force had raked out of the subconscious heap.

There was no doubt, it had become part of the texture of his mind. The girl was more real than many people he had met. Surely not more real, though, than this one who was now struggling to push him away, her eyes bright with sudden anger.

There was only one convincing thing to do and by not doing it, he gave her new proof of a divided mind. She fairly tore herself free and was climbing down through the hatch before he could stop her. Even then it was not too late and he could have got her back. But as he moved to do that thing, with his mind fully made up, the intercom on the gunnery console made an urgent play for attention. The habits of a life-time died hard and he spun round to grab the extension mike and say in a voice almost snarling with impatience, 'Fletcher. What is it?'

Bruce Charlton's genial, freckled mug on the miniature screen was a reproach in itself, and brought him back to full operational strength.

Charlton said, 'Something you'd like to know, Commander. There seems to be a fluctuation on that incoming signal. In fact it's dying on us. Rooney fixed a cathode eye in the circuit to give visual tuning for exact compensation. We can meet it now on under Mark 1. Correction. No signal. It's clear.'

'I'll check that.'

Dag swung himself round to the direct vision port. The view was now as at first. Bare green stone on the floor of their narrow cutting.

'You're right, Bruce. That was a smart move by Rooney. Give it a log entry.'

'Of course there's no guarantee that it won't come back.'

'Get hold of Rooney and put him to work on the trolley. I want a tuning eye in that circuit. It might be very important to know when we could be free to move about.'

'Cathode eye on the trolley, check.'

'I'll be rounding up Cormac now. I'd like to move out as soon as we can whilst it's clear.'

Tamar had disappeared again; but his personal affairs would have to wait, as indeed they had often had to in the past. She knew the drill, this was not by any means a first mission and she was basically fair enough to credit him with right motives. Once, he had asked her to marry him and she had refused because of their careers. This time, at the end of the trip, he would not take no for an answer. If she wanted to stay on in the service, she could take a berth in the training wing, where her experience and knowledge would be invaluable.

When he saw her again, in the wardroom for a quick meal, she was, seemingly, back to normal; keeping a seat for him next to her own, and being obliging and feminine about the choice of dishes from the well stocked dispenser. He met her in the same spirit. It was a kind of truce.

Cormac was glad to be involved. His squat powerful frame was hung around like a Christmas tree with useful Venusian bric-a-brac. He looked like a throw-back to a Wellsian eccentric professor; but there was nothing mild and inoffensive about the equipment. Unless they were going to meet something very advanced, indeed, he had enough power locked in his deep oblong harness pouches to put the I.G.O. case in an unanswerable brief.

Bruce Campbell had improvised a light unbreakable line to pay out from a belt reel. The morning's excursion had given him several ideas for improving the trolley as an extended survey vehicle. He had been working with Rooney to fit some elementary seating and storage lockers for food supplies.

Dag assembled his party on the green stone clearing and they settled themselves on the remodelled trolley. Bruce Charlton, in the continued absence of the beam, accompanied them for a last minute briefing. As they looked back at *Interstellar X* in its silo, a further thought struck his Commander.

'Another thing, Bruce, get somebody working on that white deposit on the ship. With platinum at 195 or so atomic weight, it could give us a whole new set of handling characteristics. Collect the scrapings, it might pay for the trouble.'

'Check. And on the other matter, I give you four days from now and then take off and call in the bloodhounds.'

'That's correct. Leave precisely at dusk on that day. I've logged the time for you, and if there's any suggestion of armed interference get out of it, but quick. We can't be any worse off than we'll be if we haven't reported back in that time.'

Charlton felt that the first survey party could be spared without a pang; but looking now at Fletcher, tall and bronzed in white drill, Tamar Kelly, trimly elegant in her favourite pale turquoise shirt and white pants, Cormac faintly ridiculous, but dourly determined and Campbell, pleased with himself and his ingenuity, at the controls, he knew that it would be a very hard decision to make, if he was faced with taking the ship up without them. He watched them to the head of the valley and saw Campbell take the trolley at a run up the opposing bank of shifting fibre. Then he was climbing down to the freight lift. He was ten yards from it, before the scene dissolved for him into a long vista of grey dust and he was back in the private hell of an ill-fated mission of way back.

Charlton kept going until he ran into the near tripod of his ship and worked it out doggedly in a kind of double think at two levels of awareness. His eyes had short circuited on to a vision of bleak volcanic ash. He felt again the black bitterness of that time. His miscalculation had put them there, but no one was blaming him and it now looked as though they would never find the ship again. He could not see his companions and he was trying to work out whether he was now alone or whether there were other figures still stumbling through the dust.

By touch and by a pre-set determination which was driving him on, he had found the hoist and was going up. When his mind cleared, he was looking at Freya Burleigh.

She said anxiously, 'Are you all right, Bruce?'

Curtly for him, he said, 'Well enough. That damned beam's on again. Alert Rooney.'

Four hours running on virtually a straight line course reeled off two hundred and seven kilometres. After crossing some patches of clear ground where a thin, pale soil supported clusters of flat, plate-sized, fungoid growths, they were back on the springy upland of fibrous pipeline. Trial cuttings of the one inch diameter tubes showed a narrow central capillary surrounded by grey pulpy flesh. The flow of liquid syphoned on for a few seconds and then the tube appeared to close itself.

'What kind of life is that?' Tamar was clearly getting bored with the whole setup. 'What does it *do*, anyway?'

Cormac, who was never far away from her and always watched everything she did, was the only one to answer. 'If you compare it, as a life form, with your very colourful self, no doubt you will find it hard to justify its biological place. But we do not know the whole story. Something very special indeed is managing affairs on this planet and I have no doubt, no doubt at all, that it serves some very necessary purpose. On the face of it, I would say that it was set up to carry liquid in circulation in some way. For that it is ideally suited. What is better than a living pipeline, which will maintain itself at no cost to its operator?'

Much conversation may be as good as a home; but Tamar had not bargained for her simple rhetoric to be taken up at any length. However, she was a well brought up girl, and said she thought he might very well be right at that, determining privately to keep her big mouth shut when puzzled again.

Dag said, 'I'd like to run the line down another few kilometres before the light goes. Then we can take a spell.'

Twenty minutes and almost twenty kilometres further on, it was clear that the scenery was slowly changing. For one thing they were moving parallel with the line of the never ending tubes. Anything but a tracked vehicle would not have

made any progress at all. Also they were dropping down between two banks of the piping. It was thinning out on their
line of progress until the tracks finally bit down into a bare
grey pumice which set up a dust cloud to hang like a troubled
wake behind them.

Campbell said, 'There's an increase in pressure, Commander,
as though we were dropping down to sea level.' He had already
made three upward adjustments of the protecting force field,
which was now working at seventy per cent of total available
power.

'Let's get on then and see what we're getting into.'

Horizons shrank to the skyline of the low range on either
side and the dropping curve of the lane ahead.

Tamar said, 'It's like one of those village streets that you
get in, where the sea is at the bottom of the hill and you seem
to be walking out into the sky.'

Two minutes later, Dag said reluctantly, 'Whatever lies
ahead will have to wait. It'll be dark in five minutes. Camp
now, whilst we can see we're in a fair place.'

Tamar lit a cigarette and, exceptionally for her, took the
feminine privilege of watching the unskilled labour force put
up the dome. It was tricky, in so far as the power field only
gave them a working area of one metre round the trolley itself
and the dome lay in flat sections on the trolley floor. Once in
position, its reflector plating would be as effective as the skin
of the ship in opposing the beam. But getting it assembled,
without moving out, was beginning to look like something out
of early vaudeville.

Campbell, holding one side of the unfolding base was in-
exorably edged out of the safety zone into his private Yorkshire world and stool like a post, deaf to any further appeal.
Automatic clipping devices on the underside, had already
engaged to make the structure rigid. In the green light, on the
stark set, it had a surrealist quality which appealed to Tamar.
A silver octagon with a dour gnome, a zombie and a bronzed,
lanky bean pole. She began to clap with unaffected delight,

took a step back, to view the scene with greater detachment and found herself on the empty paddock of her Cheshire farm.

Dag Fletcher supported his end with one hand and crawled underneath to hook himself on to the line from the trolley and then nodded to Cormac to move. If they all went outside the fence, he would just have to dig them out one at a time. Cormac and Campbell were moving as the structure pushed them, beyond the reach of any verbal instruction. As soon as they were on clear ground, uncluttered by offloaded stores, he stopped and put down his end. Then he set himself to think a rigid pattern of movement that might persist whatever else happened to his mind and went into the private world of Plantos Three, following the edge of the base with his fingers. When he reached Campbell, he prised the man's fingers free from their hold and lowered that edge. Then such was the preset determination of his mind, that he followed the edge back into the clear pulling Campbell after him.

After that it was relatively easy. With Campbell handling the line, he brought in Cormac and then they moved the trolley, so that its power shield overlapped the entrance of the rapidly growing, self-inflating dome.

When he brought Tamar in, the dome was complete and the racing twilight was bringing down the green light in a smooth run. She flicked away her cigarette and its glowing end made an arc of red against a dark backdrop. Dag said, 'In you go, Tamar. Tell me what it's like inside.'

When her reply came out, the husky voice pitched on a note of mock surprise, it was clear the reflectors were working. She said, 'Believe it or not, but it's *octagonal*, just like outside.'

Something about the oppressive darkness surrounding their small pool of light kept them silent through the meal. Moving on would be possible at reduced speed, but Dag estimated that a break now would pay off. He took the first watch period himself and spent two hours uneventfully sitting on the trolley or moving round the restricted site. Nothing changed except the star pattern as banks of high cloud drifted across.

At 2100 hours, he wakened Tamar. He noticed that she had sited her sleeping bag between Campbell and the ridge of the entrance lock. They were not using that clumsy atmosphere filter and had not assembled the tunnel structure; but on the floor there was a mass of clips and he would be forced to go on the far side next to Cormac. So the truce was only at surface level. Well, there would be time to sort that out.

Sleeping, her bell of red-gold hair was spread in a silky fan over the head rest. She was relaxed, utterly vulnerable; it was unbelievable that she could be an efficient and experienced executive. He wakened her by taking the hand that lay outside the cover and pressing it. She was instantly alert.

'My duty?'

'Yes. But I hardly had the heart to tell you. You look very beautiful asleep.'

'Fine speeches will get you nowhere.'

She wriggled lithely out and grabbed his arm to pull herself upright. They went outside to the trolley.

Dag said, 'There's nothing going on. Run the searchlight round every ten minutes or so.'

'It looks lighter due North.'

There was an indistinct pallor, a suggestion of *terre verte* over the horizon dead ahead.

'Could be a star cluster just out of sight.'

'It looks like a distant town. You get a lightening of the sky like that, when you're walking at night on moorland and there's a town down in a valley, miles away.'

'True, but that's the less likely explanation.'

'Those clouds, Dag.'

'What about them?'

'They have a familiar look.'

Even as they watched, the high, indeterminate outlines, there was a suggestion of suffused colour, a hint of red and deeper black against the prevailing black green. A vortex.

Forms locked in combat. He said, 'It reminds me of a picture. In your cabin surely? Franz Marc. Fighting Forms.'

Hitting the jackpot of recognition ought to have earned him a bonus; instead he got an incredulous look as the identification registered.

'Of course, Vanora brought it in. It was over her bed. You *would* remember it.'

'I ought to knock some sense into you.'

'Take care. The regulations are very explicit on that kind of behaviour. I could have you put in irons for the rest of the mission. Actually, it would be about the safest place for you to be.'

He had, however, stopped listening and was concentrating on the phenomenon above. 'There is an intelligence controlling that, and doing it from a knowledge of Vanora's mind or somebody's—who knows the picture.'

'That, I should imagine, could be any male member of the crew.'

'For God's sake, Tamar, stop being bitchy about Vanora. Anyway, it gives you something to look at. Call me at once if there's any change. No clever, independent stuff about seeing it through single-handed. That way we could all die.'

'Thank you very much, I know my duty.'

Dag was tired of the verbal fencing. He simply said, 'Goodnight then,' and disappeared through the triangular entry slit of the dome.

Tamar Kelly watched him go with mixed feelings. There was a repressive atmosphere about this place which was making her irritable. But she knew she was being unreasonable and was tempted to follow him through and make peace. Then she said aloud, 'I'm damned if I will, he'll have to earn it.' Since this decision contributed nothing to her happiness, she realised that it was probably a wrong one; but now the good moment had gone, so she paced round the clear circle and then sat on the trolley looking forward down the trough.

The rolling cloud formations held their display for another

ten minutes, then blew clear; so that dim green stars made a definitive outline of the valley.

It was not until the last half hour of her watch that she was convinced that the rising banks of vegetation on either side were nearer in, moving very slowly on to them like shifting dunes.

At first she thought it was a subjective thing. She had been looking down the valley and the sides seemed to press claustrophobically round her. But when she swung the narrow beam searchlight on its gimbal mounting, there was no doubt at all that the circular splash of light on the rising mass of creepers was much bigger in diameter than it had been. They were certainly nearer in.

Dag Fletcher was lying completely relaxed, as though he was sleeping in a bunk on Earth base. The unguarded quality of the sleeper touched her heart and made her resolve to be much nicer to him. A streak of grey in his fair hair over the left temple was a relic of some traumatic experience which he would never discuss. She knelt beside him and put out a hand to smooth it away from his forehead; but before ever it reached its objective, he was wide awake and had her wrist in a bone crushing grip.

Recognition followed so swiftly that the pressure was almost instantly taken off, but he carried the hand to his lips.

'Your servant, ma'am.'

'What a suave way to wake up.'

'What is it?'

'The creeper seems to be closing in.'

He was outside in two quick strides and swinging the lamp to check for himself.

'There isn't any doubt. Get the others up.'

Now their valley was less than a hundred metres across and the lianas were forming a steeper edge against them. In fact, with the light concentrated on one spot, he could see the dark green tubes slowly pulling and slackening, as if gigantic distant weavers were pulling warp threads on an immense loom. He was reproaching himself for not taking more care. They were in a trap. The lines had separated to let them through and they had walked into the net. Now they could not get out before it closed.

Tamar was back beside him.

'Is this what happened to the survey party?'

'Hardly, the car wouldn't be caught this way.'

'At night perhaps?'

'Heald would see to a proper watch.'

Cormac and Campbell were looking along the beam of light. Cormac said, 'So, Commander, this force is taking positive action to destroy us without listening to anything we may say.'

'It's looked into our minds, remember; perhaps it doesn't like what it sees.'

'That's not surprising.' Tamar could not resist the opening.

Dag had come to a conclusion. 'At the rate it moves, we have a little time. We need all the equipment we have. Pack up the dome, prepare to move out. We'll get the trolley on top of the hill one way or another.'

By the time the dome was in and the stores fitted over it on the small platform, there was no doubt at all of the intention behind the dark moving mass. They were in a narrowing canyon with walls going up fifteen metres to a bulging over-hang which was preparing to roll in and fill the gap.

Dag took the controls and Tamar instinctively moved closer to him on the small platform. Then they were tearing into the narrowing gap with the searchlight beam probing a thousand metres ahead.

Movement of the strands was slow and deliberate. Shift, pause and settle in the new position, with the long pipes find-ing a precarious stability in a formation which was not their natural curve of rest. Dag knew that there would have been no time to go back, the question resolved itself into what lay ahead.

Nothing encouraging, it seemed. The trolley was rocking

along at an all out seventy-five kilometres an hour. Although used to the fantastic speeds of space travel in a theoretical sense, they had seldom had such direct experience of speed. Tamar found it exhilarating. Breath crammed at her nose and throat, hair flying back like a golden pennant, holding on to the low tubular hoop.

Then they were tearing between cliffs not twenty metres apart, with the beam lost in the narrowing mass ahead. Above them a thickening cornice was preparing to roll down and plug the gap.

Cormac heaved himself forward and beat on Dag's shoulder to get attention. He had anticipated the next move by a split second. Fletcher was already cutting back to bring the trolley to a halt. The Venusian had pitched his voice to a shout and it cracked into the sudden silence like a madman's outburst.

'Commander. We must try an explosive force.'

Dag was already ferreting in the equipment box at his feet. He had hoped to find a way out by climbing the side; but clearly that would not serve. Blasting out a path would possibly create as many problems as it solved, but it was the only thing left.

Cormac was already fitting a slim, six inch, grey shaft like a quarrel bolt into a small spring loading arbalest which assembled from one of the many do-it-yourself kits hung round his harness.

'Allow me, Commander,' his voice dropped again into a throaty croak, 'I shall have to make the report about use of a nuclear force in any event.'

It was a point. Justification for use of one of the major weapons would come best from the resident I.G.O. commissar. Dag said, 'Into the left bank, then. About sixty metres ahead.'

The quarrel bolt shone briefly in the staring light of their lamp, then it disappeared into the migratory tubes. For ten seconds, there was anti-climax. Silence after the rush down the lane, stillness, after hectic movement. On their right the great overhang began to droop down.

Lying flat beside the trolley, they felt the floor of the valley tilt underneath them. A hot draught funnelled past, with a stupifying roar like a rocket engine on a test bed. Hanging on, with finger tips dug into crannies of the pumice rock, Dag forced his head up to see what was going on. He saw the night sky blotted out by a great writhing mass of lianas, blown clear even as he looked up, and a whole new skyline developing.

There was a new sound, of heavy, glutinous liquid rolling towards them. He said, 'Time to go,' and was pulling Tamar to her feet. Then he was urging the machine up a long tangled slope, slippery with the contents of broken tubes, with the tracks racing and sliding until they bit down into the stable undersurface. Free ends curled out and writhed at them, depressions, filled with the pale sappy fluid, drenched them; but Dag went on, rock steady, in an all out concentration of will to get them to the top.

It was a half kilometre of tumbled confusion. Then they were back on the familiar uplands of tubing, which appeared as undisturbed as any they had travelled on. From the top of the rise, the lightening of the northern sky was a definite feature. An arc of pallor straddled the line of their course.

Dag stopped. They were all wet through; but in the prevailing warmth that was no special hardship. More trying was the weight. Even their thin clothing had become as heavy as sheet lead. In the dim, reflected light of the probing beam, Dag saw that Tamar appeared to be sheathed in a second skin of tin foil. Her hair was plastered to her head and emphasised the satisfying proportions of the golden section in all its basic architecture. Every curve of her Maillol figure was outlined in faithful detail. Body heat and the high temperature were wreathing her in a kind of diaphanous haze of rapid evaporation. He said, 'Every cloud has its silver lining,' and even as he said it, there was an echo in his mind of a conversation with Vanora. Wise at last in that direction, he kept the reference to himself; but the train of thought was enough to have him looking ahead at the distant light. He continued, 'We might just as well go on. Quite a lot of things will become clearer when we find out what's over there.'

Cormac, a squat grotesque in his layer of white deposits, said seriously, 'That is possible. But not certain. Like the boy who lost a coin and was looking for it under a lighted window. His father asked him what he was doing, and when the boy told him, he said, 'Are you sure you lost it just there?' The boy said, 'Oh no, I didn't lose it here; but this is the only place where there's a light.'

This simple piece of Venusian analysis went some way to reconcile Tamar to a character who had so far only managed to give her the creeps. She said, 'That's right. We mustn't fall into elementary errors of reasoning. I always stick to the five element syllogism myself. There are people in yonder mountain for there is a light in it. Wherever there is a light, there are people, as in a town; there is a light in the mountain, so there must be people in it.'

Dag said, 'It would be pure pleasure, of course, to listen to this gab all night; but we have a train to catch.' He took them off at a sharpish acceleration which pushed the seminarists back in their seats.

Tamar said, 'That's typical. No intellectual curiosity. Run away from anything you don't understand.'

The trolley notched up to half speed. It seemed very fast in the darkness; but the distant light was like a beacon. They fell silent and endured in heavy, stiffening clothing, feeling cold now in the slip-stream. Light grew ahead into an Aurora Borealis which lit up the undulating green dunes with a cold, **pallid glare.**

CHAPTER SIX

THIRTY kilometres of hard driving with weariness a settled thing, to be discounted like a fact of life, brought the source of diffused light into the composition. A low lying oval rim, tilted south to show them a long ellipse, filled the way ahead. Light spilled from it in a steady glare.

Dag Fletcher stopped on the top of a long undulation and they looked in silence. One element at least of Tamar's syllogism was established. Light there was.

Campbell said, 'They'd soon have reached that in the car. I suppose they'd fly over it to take a look inside.' He did not finish what he obviously meant; that, in fact, the car had been then intercepted in some way and taken down into the crater.

Fletcher moved them forward and the roller coaster ride was on again. He could not quite believe that the other party was out of action. There were design features of the scout car which would take it out of most kinds of trouble. It was engineered to cope with hostile environmental forces. Heald was no Napoleon; but he was clever enough to come in out of the rain. What else though? Tamar voiced it for him; she said, 'But the cloud formations earlier? That suggests that they are still very much alive.'

Imperceptibly at first, and then with a definite change in motion, they were moving up a long gradual gradient. It was a surprise when the tracks bit suddenly on clear ground. Dag swung the headlamp left and right to see what they were getting into. The long green creeper had separated again, to pass on lower ground round the sides of the crater. At least, it disappeared beyond the range of vision and dark masses in the distance suggested that it was doing that thing. The radiance which fanned from the crater seemed to have the curious property of being visibly light without giving its light to the surrounding countryside.

Campbell asked wearily, 'Not again?'

'I do not think so,' Cormac was the least affected by the journey and his throaty croak was as deliberative as ever. 'Whatever else, this intelligence which opposes us is of a complex nature. It would not try the same thing twice. No, I believe this is a genuine change in the terrain.'

Certainly, they were on an apron of open rock which was widening rather than narrowing. Now it was black basalt shining darkly in their dipping beam. Pressure was less, and they noticed it as a relief from an undefined malaise. There was also a very faint breeze stirring which gave a chill to the last areas of damp in their stiff white clothing.

Tamar shivered involuntarily and Campbell said, 'Somebody's walking over your grave.'

'A real friend would offer his jacket instead of saying *hic jacet*.'

'God protect me from an intellectual woman.'

'Amen to that,' said Dag, and got a well deserved hack on his left shin, with a husky injunction to watch it. He was glad enough to receive the blow as a gesture of good will. Like being beaten over the skull with an olive branch. Then they fell silent again as the trolley tilted to a climb and its engine note dropped a semi-tone. Now the light ahead was giving a twilight zone of illumination to a rugged moonscape of fantastically angled rock. Dag had to use every ounce of concentration to pick a path to take them forward.

Cormac said suddenly, 'Commander, I have been watching the sky due south. There is a very unusual star at almost thirty degrees of elevation. What do you make of it?'

Dag thought that it was just like Cormac to expect him to

look in two directions, but respected the man's sense enough to stop and take a direct look. After staring into the light, the way back appeared at first in undifferentiated black. Then he saw what Cormac was on about. The tiny speck was too roundly regular to be a distant star and Thirza had no moons or satellites of any kind.

Tamar, anticipating, handed him a small high power telescope from the instrument box. He steadied it on her shoulder and took a long look. Then he stepped aside and motioned Cormac to try his luck.

Tamar said, 'Could you see?'

'Well enough.'

'I'm glad of that. You were standing on my feet.'

'In every life a little rain must fall.' But it was absently said; because there was no doubt at all about what the star was. Cormac confirmed it without the help of Tamar as a tripod. She was beginning to see good qualities in the dour Venusian; but still felt an involuntary physical withdrawal from any close contact.

He said flatly, 'It is a military machine, a frigate, I think, and not of any fleet in the I.G.O. network. What do you say, Commander?'

'There's no doubt. O.G.A. In a parking orbit. Probably not visible from *Interstellar X*. If Charlton goes up, he'll be a sitting target.'

'Will they have sighted our ship?'

'Not necessarily; but it won't take long from there. They'll be doing a detailed scan. We'd better get on with this. Take a look over the crater and then get back.'

The trolley churned its way up a long scree and they stopped with the single eye of the searchlight making bright, concentric rings on a near vertical face of rock. Now they were in an area of penumbra, shaded from the mushroom of eerie light by the rim of the crater itself. Campbell searched round for an easy pitch, but there was none. There was only straight up and the trolley had come to the end of its run.

Tamar said, 'We can't operate usefully outside the power screen, and we can't carry the trolley.' As a statement of the obvious it was hardly worthy of the five element syllogist; but it cleared Dag's mind and a possible answer came up. They would have to use individual screens and seemingly the reflector plating of the survival dome had the right properties.

He said, 'That's true. Get the dome out. We'll dismantle it and make Ned Kelly helmets out of the pieces.'

It had not been wholly straightforward on the level. Pulling out the flat octagon was going to be good clean knockabout stuff on a three-in-one slope. Tamar said, 'Oh, Good. This, I can't wait to see.' But she reckoned without that disappointing command quality, which learns fast from error, and had to watch Fletcher and Campbell manœuvre the clumsy base in a vertical plane. However, there was sudden reaffirmation that the best precept in the human situation is 'wait and hope'. As soon as the base straightened and the locking clips engaged, the dome began its automatic inflation routine and its blunt, growing tip began to push Cormac off the trolley. He did his best to struggle away from it; but he was badly placed and cumbered with much equipment. Before Dag could grab him, he was outside the protected zone and sliding down the scree, locked in his private daydream.

Dag said, 'Zero reaction tool, Tamar. Quickly now,' and was prising out the base plates to get at the mechanism. Seconds later it began to retract in a half-hearted way and then sagged into scrap.

A section of half a dozen plates made a reasonable cowl. Campbell cut a simple pattern of slots and tongues, hooked them neatly together, and put the shiny bin on his head.

'Eye slits?'—his voice was muffled, but audible.

'Try it. After all this must kill most of the signal.'

Campbell bored two tiny holes and put it back. Vision was limited, because Tamar was trying to look in at him. Dag said, 'What can you see?'

D

'Nothing, it's dark. I don't believe there's a head inside at all.'

'For God's sake, Tamar, stop messing about. Can you see enough to move around, Dick?'

'It will serve.'

'Right, take a line and get after Cormac.'

Three steps proved the portable screen. They saw Campbell give a thumbs up signal and cast himself free of the line. Then he was sliding and stumbling down the slope to where Cormac had reached zero momentum. Minutes later, he was back in the fold leading the Venusian like a shaggy dog.

The four heads which poked themselves over the skyline had a blind, reptilian look which would have alarmed any human viewer. Tamar, ever sensitive to atmosphere, was alarmed enough herself; wearing the blank mask seemed to carry an obligation to be a ghoul. But what she saw, down a long receding slope of white, powdery sand, was enough to swamp misgivings in a rising tide of indignation.

Set in random order, facing everywhichway, perfect in each exquisite detail, white crystal statues of Vanora were multiplied on the foreground as though Praxiteles and his workshop had been bashing at it without a break over the last three millenia.

Campbell said, muffled, but incredulous, 'It's Vanora.'

Dag said, 'That must be the understatement of all time.'

'You'd better go and check them for anvil-shaped marks,' Tamar sounded resigned and disgusted. No girl ever had more unfair competition.

Cormac got himself full marks for finding nothing unusual in the nearer spectacle. He was looking over the many trim heads to a vast lagoon, which filled the centre of the crater. Dotted about its surface, fantastically shaped outcrops of white porous metal were glowing with light, the source of light, in fact, which had led them to this place.

He said, 'The principle of Dobereiner's lamp—hydrogen ignited by platinum sponge. Some reaction frees the gas from the lake and the rest is automatic. And on the far shore, we should find the answer. Only people, surely, would require buildings such as those.'

'As in a town?'

'Precisely.'

Dag broke in on this marriage of true minds. 'Tamar, stay here with the Commissar. We'll be back.'

Followed by Campbell, he heaved himself over the ridge and dropped at full arm stretch into ankle-deep sand which had the consistency of fine talc and rose in swirls as he walked forward.

The two men threaded their way across the thronged, but silent beach, raising a wake of white spirals, on a set waiting for a *prima ballerina* to enter on little feet and flee from a satyr round the statuary. Cormac would have qualified, at a superficial level, for the latter role; but would have missed his cue, because his mind was entirely taken up by speculation about the distant buildings. After a long look through his monocular, prismatic glass he said, 'Definitely Cappodanian.'

'That's hardly likely.'

'Likely or not, Lieutenant Kelly, I spent a long tour of service on Cappodan. The architectural style is unmistakable.'

'Then this planet has already been colonised by an I.G.O. people?'

'It would appear to be so.'

'But, as far as we know, Cappodan had no space research programme until very recently. The people there were not advanced technologically until they came into the I.G.O. sphere of influence. Earth Space sent a contingent to help with the education programme.'

'Again, that is so. You are very well informed. But that was over a century ago. And for centuries before that, the people were using space craft on charter. They were, and are, very much in demand as space crew. They have exceptional qualities of psychological stability. Stress syndromes are virtually unknown. It will be very interesting indeed to see what a group of Cappodanian expatriates are doing in this set-up. Very interesting indeed.'

Fletcher and Campbell had reached the water's edge without incident. It was gin-clear to the shelving bottom of white sand. They followed the line of it to the right and disappeared behind a projecting spur where the prevailing light breeze had built up a horseshoe-shaped dune. Then Campbell reappeared signalling for the other two to join the party.

When they toiled round the corner, Tamar restraining her impatience to stay with the Venusian, who was definitely not purpose-built for soft sand work, they came out on the quayside of a small harbour. Dag's shiny bin jutted out of the foreground in a way that could only mean he was walking on water or had found a boat. Tamar made framing mimes with her hands to study the composition.

She said, 'Hold it there, Dag. Smile now. Can you balance a poached egg on your left shoulder? Take one.'

He said, 'What did you say?'

The good second, if it had ever existed, had gone; she said, 'I said, "What have you got there?"'

'One guess.'

Had there been rocks about, Tamar felt she would have been well justified in dropping one on his head. But the harbour walls and the parapet were metal smooth in a continuous sheet. Slots at half metre intervals made a simple ladder and she climbed down to join him on the deck of a long punt-shaped barge, some five metres wide by fifteen long. It was decked for half its length, and the covered saloon this made was furnished like a forecastle with bunks and a long centre table.

'It's made of thin, sheet metal,' Campbell was tapping a bulkhead with the butt of his laser.

Dag said, 'We might get protection from it. I'll try it. Put my lid back, if necessary.'

Tamar tried to intervene. She suddenly thought that it was

much safer on her farm than his decorated pavement, but she was too late. In the event, there was no difficulty, he said, 'All right, you can come out. It's all clear.'

Dag Fletcher knew the value of having a rested crew and there seemed little gain to be made by moving on without some observation. There was still an hour before the notional dawn. He said, 'We'll finish that interrupted camp. Four hours; that gives us each three hours sleep. I'll take first watch.'

When he handed over to Campbell there was no change in the scene. They watched for a few minutes together, whilst the racing dawn brought a pale green flood on to the backdrop and showed them that their crater was the low point of a considerable range. Beyond the far rim, slopes covered with green, tubular creeper went up to what could be a rocky tableland. No other buildings were in sight. The collection across the lake seemed to be humanity's lot and would house a community of about a hundred or two.

When Tamar took over, last in the chain, there was some movement. Small figures could be seen on the distant shore. When she woke the other three, her conversion disc was showing 1000 hours local time, and there was general activity all along the opposite beach.

Fletcher had slept on a problem which he had not solved when it rose in his mind on their arrival. The boat was clearly meant to sail the waters of the lake, but there was no mast or provision for oars. Obviously a propulsion unit of some kind had to exist, but it was not easy to find. Cormac pottering about in the stern, found the answer. A non-return inlet valve allowed water to flow aboard into a shallow rectangular tank below the decking where a transparent top section showed enough for them to guess at the action. Water was fed through a network of fine wires which had a catalytic effect. Released gas was ignited instaneously and forced its way, by expansion, out of two fishtail jets set below water level. Directional control was simply a matter of closing off one or other of these.

At 1020 hours *Skylark* was ready for its trip round the bay. Dag said, 'I would prefer to let the people over there know that we are mainly a friendly lot; but since we can't, we shall just have to go across and tell them it is so.'

'How do you look friendly in one of these?' Tamar tapped his helmet.

'Mime it.'

'Like this?' She went through the traditional ballet sequence of hand movement for 'come dance with me'.

'That will be very effective. But God alone knows what it might mean to a Cappodanian.'

'I hope they give me time.'

'Looking as you do, I should think there's likely to be an enthusiastic rush.'

The punt was nosing out of its quay and met the gentle swell of the open lake. It was almost silent in operation, only a faint hiss came from the pushing gas. Central in the flat bottom, an inspection panel showed the white floor of the crater receding in a three in one slope. When they were a kilometre out it was a pale blur at great depth.

Standing in the stern, Campbell steered a direct course across the centre. Distance was deceptive, after fifteen minutes they appeared to be very little nearer. Tamar knelt in the well looking down through the transparent flooring; Maillol's 'Kneeling Girl' with her head in a bucket. Suddenly she called out, 'Oh, no!'

Dag Fletcher came from under the forecastle cover to join her.

'What is it?'

'That ubiquitous creep.'

'Vanora?'

'Is there another?'

He let it go. Certainly the sight below would only have pleased a determined fan. The bottom was now covered by a pale, translucent, green crystalline form. They were crossing its lower slopes. If it were regular in shape, it would balance the incline of the crater and rise almost to the surface of the water in the centre. And in that event it would be gigantic. On land it would dwarf the Great Pyramid. But physical marvels were no novelty, what gave this one its distinction was that each one of the myriad facets, now in view, was mirroring a small, perfect picture of Vanora.

'Wouldn't it make you sick?'

Tamar was disappointed in not receiving any ready or enthusiastic agreement. Whatever the reservations, few could look at the miniature Fingalnan without delight that the human form could achieve such exquisite proportions. She left the viewing port and went into the forecastle; there she took off her tin can and shook out her hair as one whose patience has had its last knock. Then she looked ahead through a thick quartz-like window in the bows which, they had already discovered, had similar screening properties to the metal itself. Nothing was happening on the far shore. This negative observation at first made no impact, then she realised it could have meaning.

'Dag.'

'What is it, then?'

'Tear yourself away and take a look out here.'

'So, it's a tea break.'

'I suppose so. But it's a bit of a change. They have been beaver busy up to just now.'

'Doing what? Did you notice that?'

'Not really. They seemed to be doing a mammoth sand cleaning job. Collecting it, sifting it. They've cleared all their gear back to the compound.'

'Above the tide line.'

'You could say that if it were tidal water.'

'Well, we'll be a long time yet before we arrive. By that time, they may be back.'

Cormac had joined them inside. He said, 'I believe the force of the beam is becoming a good deal stronger. Twice, I have had to concentrate very hard to keep my mind on the present and on the situation here. We are moving to the centre of this crystal form and the greatest strength will be there. Perhaps we should take a more roundabout route.'

Whatever course change Dag might have made, was, however, suddenly an academic question. Campbell said, 'There's a current here. I can't make it straight across. We're being taken to starboard even with full corrective thrust.'

Now the smooth surface of the lake showed the developing power of the movement from below. A circular whirlpool effect was building up, raising the water level at the rim and depressing the centre, so that the tip of the vast crystal was revealed as a slender, fluted column of pale green.

This was now the only part of the crystal to be visible. A milky white precipitate was boiling up from below, clouding the whole lake.

Although the motion of the boat was still rock steady, its speed, measured against the static background of the mountains, was notching up. They went at the speed of the whole body of water, a leaf in a gathering whirlpool. Through the inspection window in the bottom, Cormac stared into the opaque cloud and then called, 'Commander! This may well be a recurrent phenomenon. In which case, it may be the cause of the temporary eclipse of the beam influence.'

Before Dag could reply he had made the practical experiment of taking off his protective cowl and was able to carry on with, 'Indeed it is so. That means at least half an hour of freedom to act.'

It became immediately apparent that this was in fact one of those freedoms which are theoretical rather than real. They were slowly sliding from the rim of the great vortex towards its dished centre, where the exposed column stood like a bearing shaft.

Dag Fletcher joined Campbell in the stern. Even without the cowls, speech was getting difficult in the tearing wind of their passage. He shouted, 'Keep her head up.' But his gesture was plainer than the words. Campbell was already giving full power to the compensating jet, and they were still falling off. Speed was to some extent keeping them out of the centre, but water was now in a white hurrying hill to port and dropped away to a three in one slope to starboard.

Tamar stumbled back to join them and Dag suddenly realised that the four bodies might be deployed as a sail. It was too much to explain, so he simply pushed her to the rail, put his lips to her right ear and said, 'Stay put.' His mind raced over the multiple calculations of wind force, areas, likely pressures. It was interesting, but only capable of approximate assessment. There were too many imponderables. Cormac was stationed, dour and solid next in line. Then he took the end. He had slanted the file and the wind pushed on it like an arrow in a parallelogram of forces. Campbell was shouting something which was inaudible, but the head began to lift. Then they were even clawing up to the top rim of the whirlpool.

Heads poking over the milky wall, they watched the shore, with its village complex set back behind a white boundary wall, hurtle past like a pasteboard cut out on the route of a scenic railway. Then they were going back to their starting point. One thing was clear enough, there was suddenly a great deal more water in the lake. Most of the beach where they had embarked was under water and the statues of Vanora had disappeared.

They circled again, hanging on with every last ounce of strength to a small shred of determined policy in a world reduced to an elementary chaos of wind and water. Spray from the blunt foot of the craft made a drenching curtain that sealed them in to their narrow world of noise and strain. It added to what had been shipped over the side and slopped about the bilges with a weighty run that could take them over.

Second time for the village, and the purpose of the shielding embankment was made obvious as the milky froth edged up to

its base works. Back in the same tearing haste to their starting point. There was a difference developing in the feel of
the boat under their feet. It was labouring along, slowing,
with a wave piling up at the stern. When it broke over the
transom Campbell was knocked flat and washed forward into
the forecastle. Cormac kept his feet like a squat post, integral
with the boat's fabric. Tamar, nearest the rail, lost her footing and was over the side before Dag could move.

She felt the change as a relief. Floating buoyantly on the
dense white cushion of water was a relaxation after the long
muscular strain of bracing upright against the gale. At water
level there was no pressure from the wind, she was carried
along on the moving surface. She was not afraid and had no
thought that she had reached any special crisis. If this was
drowning it was very comfortable; but even that was hardly
formulated as a definite gloss on the situation when Dag
Fletcher appeared beside her and grabbed her firmly round
the waist. Her head dipped momentarily below the surface
and she could only regard it as a change for the worse.

He had moved as her heels went neatly over the side, thinking it out as he went to follow her. If the line on his belt had
not hooked on the rail as he went over, he would have gone
over in any case. But it did and he reached her with a couple
of metres in hand. Even as his grip tightened, the speeding
boat took up the slack and they were jerked forward in its
wake.

Tamar was finding it hard to be grateful. She automatically
locked her arms round him and for some minutes they trailed
like a bulky drogue pulling the boat crabwise against its
course. When he found time to force his head against the
pushing water and kiss her lips, it was a conciliatory move, a
momentary strenuous sweetness which carried its perils as
being almost a kiss of death. But she endured suffocation
long enough for her answering pressure to be a clear affirma-
tive and then they both concentrated on keeping their heads
over the bow wave they were piling up.

Cormac brought them in. Campbell had not come out of the bunkhouse. He had been brought up by a stanchion and was lying head and shoulders in a bunk with his legs washing about in the swirling white water. The Venusian had enormous strength in his wide shoulders and pulled in the line a metre at a time, tying off each loop at the rail. When they were alongside, he leaned down and heaved them in a straight lift until Dag could grab the side and take some of the weight.

They met Campbell, crawling on hands and knees out of the forecastle. He and Fletcher arrived at the tiller in the same instant of time with *Skylark* dropping away down the tundish on a collision course for its centrepiece. Between them they checked the run, but nothing was going to take them back on top. They were wallowing now with the freeboard halved and another following wave building up to take them on the starboard quarter.

Powerless to change anything, they hung on and once more the wave broke. Now the boat was virtually awash with no steerage problem, because there was no response at all to the manipulation of the jets. A screening helmet bobbed out of the depths of the forecastle, and Tamar waded thigh deep to grab it, then she began to bale.

Fletcher and Campbell, moving by touch and memory in the heavy opaque milk bath, found two more and joined her. It was an illustration that one need not hope in order to work.

Now they were only a hundred metres from the column and if they contrived to miss it there was only a sliding hill of water to hit which must engulf them. At this distance, the column appeared to glow with an inner light. It radiated a kind of prescience. Dag paused in his chore for a brief direct look and was suddenly and inexplicably aware that it *knew* about them and that the convulsion of the lake was an organised thing which was connected with its inner life. He saw that Cormac was gripping the coaming of the forecastle deck

and staring fixedly into the pale green crystal. He too had in-
terpreted what was going on.

His attention was taken by a new movement in the water.
The pillar appeared to be shrinking, but he then realised it
was the water which was rising. As suddenly as it began,
the phenomenon was ending and the great funnel was filling
up. When they crossed the centre, the column was covered
and in the sudden quiet, Campbell's voice appeared to shout,
'Missed it, for a goddamned miracle.'

But he spoke just under a second early. Weighted down
as it was, the tin barge was drawing a good two metres at the
stern and the crystal peak caught it a grinding blow under
Fletcher's feet. He felt the skin buckling beneath him and
hurled himself forward into the water in the waist, taking
Tamar down with him in an involuntary flying tackle.

As they surfaced and he helped her to her feet, she said
huskily, 'Aren't you taking it a bit far? I forgive you. Cross
my heart. You can pack in all this diving about.' Then she
saw the stern beginning to dip and began to bale again although she was aching in every joint.

Campbell had restarted the jets and they were dead straight
for the village. Instead of a reconnaissance to find out what
went on there, it was now a matter of reaching that beach,
because it was the nearest and the only slim hope of safety.
But with three balers, then two as one of the helmets disin-
tegrated into scrap, their freeboard was a diminishing asset
and the *Skylark's* options ran out.

Tamar said, between weary movements, 'It's like . . .
those . . . God forsaken questions . . . about one pipe filling
a tank in . . . nine minutes . . . and one emptying it in nine
and a half. I never really . . . believed it.'

Proof, however, of the intractable nature of the problem
was not far away. There was a heavy lurching movement
and the metal hull fell away from their feet.

The change was in some ways an amelioration of their
lot. Whilst the boat was technically afloat, they had to try.

Now they had only their own bodies to think about and in the high density liquid, even a non-swimmer would have had to work at it to drown. There was over a kilometre to go. Dag shepherded them into a diamond formation, hooked together by unbreakable line, with himself at the leading point, Tamar and Campbell on the wings and Cormac, a sluggish, half tide rock, in the rear. Then they were moving forward again in a clumsy crawl through thin treacle.

The white suspension was dropping away and the water was glass clear down to the sinking cloud. Even at that, it had buoyancy plus and a long swim was not much problem. The upper slopes of crystal came into view, clear now of images of Vanora, much to Tamar's relief. Struggling in an uncouth muddle over a million or two cool pictures of the snide perfectionist would have been to drink the last bitter dregs of humiliation. But like the others, Tamar could not avoid looking at the great glowing facets of the crystal, and like them she became aware that it was, in a real sense, alive and conscious of their presence.

They were swimming now, automatically to a rhythm, each one silent and walled in his own world of thought. The slopes of crystal were clear to the limits of vision and Dag remembered the previous period when the outgoing, mind-bending beam had been in abeyance. No doubt this was a regular phenomenon. The locals had clearly expected it. So it came, clouded the crystal, and passed. That bit of free association dredged up the knowledge of what happened next. Of course, the outgoing influence would start up again. And they were sitting ducks for it.

Before he could pass on these fruits of research, he was back in the centre of the mosaic pavement of the underground city on Plantos Three. There was the girl, smiling up at him. It was a kind of homecoming. But his mind had also locked itself in a pattern of effort and he went on swimming, unaware that he was so doing, and unaware that he was virtually towing three human logs behind him. Tamar had dropped thankfully on the lush grass of the paddock in front of her Cheshire home. Campbell was on the lawn before GREY STONES. Cormac had delved back into his stark Venusian past. Time was no longer a meaningful measure of changing circumstance.

CHAPTER SEVEN

CONSCIOUSNESS of the here and now was soured for Dag Fletcher by an all-consuming ache. He was first aware that his shoulders and arms stretched out in front of his head were shot through with needles of cramp. The only aspect of the situation which was reading a measure of continuity was the pavement. He was lying on a tiled, ceramic floor. But it was plain and undecorated. His laughing girl was gone.

Caution was an ingrained habit, and in spite of the pain he gave no indication that he had rejoined the contemporary scene. For one thing, his mind, racing to catch up, told him that he had been brought to this place by some other agency than his own will, and anyone who wanted to shower him with the minor courtesies would have seen him more comfortably settled. Then the timing too. Experience showed that there was almost twenty hours between the periods of suspension of the mind-blocking beam. His limbs told him that he had been lying like this for a long time and it could be that long.

Where then would Tamar and the others be? Even as the question came into mind, he realised that he had not thought first about the girl. Had he done so, he might have moved automatically to look for her. Perhaps at some deep psychological level there was a list of priorities; survival number one; affection second? Or duty or honour or desire for power? It was no clear issue at that. In a way, it was diminishing to personality that it was so. It was not even possible to make a good gesture. He saw all his fantastic endeavours on a chemist's balance and weighed against them a diminutive

111

golden replica of Tamar Kelly, poised like a diving trophy. He depressed the lever which brought the arm of the balance on to its fulcrum; but before the evaluation could take effect, a voice separated out of the introspective swamp.

It was unmistakably Vernon Spencer's and it said, 'The lake's started its nonsense again; so any minute now we should hear Fletcher sounding off. But after the hours he's spent on the floor there, he won't be madly keen to leap about and it won't be long before he goes under again.'

That was a point. There was not long to do anything that could be done. He knew without any elaborate check that all his equipment had gone. So he was virtually unarmed. So there was little point in doing anything except take a look.

With a total concentration of will, he gathered his body for an all-out effort. He wanted to be on his feet before anyone did anything at all. It was a fairly impressive performance, even with stiff and reluctant muscles damping his reflexes to several multiples of their norm. Then he was standing with his back against a wall of large, metre square slabs and looking round a small, lofty room which was completely empty.

The anticlimax was so surprising, that he did nothing for some seconds, sorting out the various agonies of arms and shoulders and thighs. There appeared to be no door; but a grille of white metal went from just over head height to ceiling level across the whole width of the facing wall. It was from there Spencer had spoken and Vanora's voice confirmed it. She said, 'I would like to know, Vernon, what the instwuctions are for *Interstellar X*. If Charlton has been told to leave at a certain time, we should know what it is. So you had better get the good commander out of it and ask him.'

'That could have been done at any time with one of the screening helmets.'

'I don't place much weliance on it, but the discomfort might have made him easier to talk to. Anyway, I'm sure he will tell us; if you bwing in that wed girl and push her about.'

'A pleasure.'

'In this instance it is puwely a business matter. Your pleasure will have to wait.'

There was no mistaking the executive quality in the Fingalnian's tone. Even with the lisp. But Spencer was no easy subordinate, even in a cause of his own choosing. Vanora's voice changed and became very appealing indeed. 'No, Vernon. I'll never forgive you, you'll pay for it. Stop it.' Now there was a note of real anxiety which suddenly hit a pure G in alt., as she qualified for inclusion in any roll call of prima donnas with a brief, musical scream.

Fletcher took some small encouragement, not for the first time, in the knowledge that once beyond the rule of law, the opposition tended to spend itself in forming splinter groups. Those who could not accept one discipline were usually unable to accept another. He had already moved across the small cell and had hooked his fingers on the ledge below the grille. Pulling up was one of the most painful pieces of self-inflicted torture he had ever endured; but the view over the edge went some way to compensate.

Spencer was making it clear to Vanora that he was nobody's errand boy. A small, ladylike looking laser on the tiled floor could well have been once in her possession. She looked as though she would have liked to use it now. Facing the grille, she was making no effort to conceal her loathing for the man who held her casually under his arm. No amount of contortion could actually make her face other than beautiful; but her green eyes were bright and fairly snapping with anger. He would do well to take care not to turn his back on her in future.

This consideration seemed, however, not to weigh at all with Spencer. He brought his free hand down hard and flat on the taut seat of her pants, three times for luck and Fletcher saw that the first reaction from the victim was one of utter amazement. It could not have happened before.

Spencer set her down on her feet and patted her head,

which, like his own, was neatly covered in a shiny white helmet. Then he picked up the laser and put it in her hand.
'Now we'll see about Fletcher. But don't push me Vanora and
we'll get along very well.'

He was walking to the grille and Dag dropped the half
metre to ground level with a picture on his retina of Vanora
lifting the laser to drill a little hole in the man's back. The
fact that, seconds later the mesh was pulled away and he
leaned through, head and shoulders, was the proof that she
was woman enough to change her mind.

There was not much to be gained by anything but direct
dealing. Dag said, 'So you got here, Spencer. Give me a hand
out of this.' He held up his right hand for Spencer to grip.

Even as Spencer leaned further down to take his arm in
a locking wrist grip, Dag knew that with Vanora above it
could only end one way. But he had to try. As the grip
tightened, he used the suspended arm like a swinging rope
and lifted his whole weight from the ground on to it. Then he
planted his feet wide apart on the facing wall and heaved.
Spencer came into the apartment like a yo-yo on a fast return.
In one aspect, he had come up to standard on training grades,
his reflexes were very fast and he made a model forward
roll landing which brought him to his feet, so that he was
moving towards Fletcher as he stiffly came round to meet
him.

It did him no good. Dag was seeing in him a tangible, ex-
ternalised expression of all the complications of the mission.
A direct opponent of that rule of law which he believed instinctively was the only sure foundation of human values.
Physical action was a welcome relief. Before Spencer had time
to exploit the initiative, he found himself in a bone-crushing
lock which threatened to lift his head off.

When the pressure suddenly eased and Fletcher's dead
weight fell against him, he thought for a moment it was
a trick to get him to move into some new area of agony and
waited for the next thing. This proved to be Vanora's voice,

which said, 'Just push him away, Vernon, and let him fall.'

'You took your time.' Spencer was gingerly feeling his neck. 'And any questions are now definitely out. On the whole, your interventions are very clumsy for a professional agent. You make me nervous about the success of our enterprise. Well, back up top.' Any overture of gratitude seemed to be missing, but she took it without comment and submissively allowed him to lift her up to the open grille. Then she turned and helped him through. There was more strength in her lightweight, athlete's body than anyone would expect.

As the metal guard pivoted back, Fletcher was seeing the floor again and though he could not have told how long he had been out, he knew he was still within the period of the mind's eclipse. It always took a long time to get him thoroughly angry. Mostly, he had to simulate even testiness as a gimmick to impress training personnel. But the series of events, which now had him looking at this ceramic pad for a second time, had some irritating features which were slowly turning him to cold homicidal fury.

For one thing, he was blaming himself and that was a prime stimulus for moving outwards to look for someone to cleave into faggots. Vanora's callous disregard in placing her bombs; the mind-bender's stupid, repetitive, but successful trick of blanking them out into private hallucination, suddenly made him feel that someone was treating him as a child. But when he reached the ledge once more, the grille was secured and the room beyond it was empty.

He pulled himself up and stood on the three centimetre lip with his fingers hooked in the mesh and looked around. There was not a lot to see. An oblong room with its long axis running away from him to a blank wall. One opening up stage left, without a visible door. Smallish. That gelled with Cormac's view about Cappodanian architecture. They were a people of small stature. One point five metres average height. Whilst these facts registered and ticked themselves off, his fingers were exploring the metal work. It could hardly be more simple. Whatever control dropped the lugs to release the frame and allow it to swivel on centre pivots, was just beyond the reach of his probing fingers. Probably top dead centre.

Lift it then? Crouched, because of the ceiling, edged on a narrow foothold, he found he could only apply a fraction of his strength. Even then he lifted the whole grille until it baulked against the roof with a good centimetre to go before it rose clear of the holding grooves.

He dropped down to floor level and took off his left epaulette. In the stiffening of the overstitched seams was a six centimetre length of serrated infrangom. It would certainly cut the metal above, but it would take time. Whether or not there would be enough of that bent commodity, before the crystal sorted itself out, was just another imponderable.

He had been working for five minutes when the empty set began to fill up. Two Cappodanians came on from some invisible entrance down stage, right. They were in national costume, dark brown, round necked singlets with a kind of kilt in the same material, pleated at the sides with plain panels front and rear. Small dark men with a high cephalic index. Heads in fact almost spherical—a trait emphasised by hemispheres of white metal fitting like skull caps. That was a point. So they had organised themselves to live under the shadow of the crystal.

They looked at him without much curiosity, seemingly secure in the knowledge that although he might choose an eccentrically uncomfortable perch, he couldn't get out. Vanora was next in line, then Tamar Kelly, very pale and wide eyed, with her arms straight at her sides because they were on the inside of a broad metal belt which was clipped tightly round her middle like a straitjacket. Spencer was prodding her forward with the end of a thin flexible rod and Heald made an apologetic looking, tail end Charlie. All God's children except Tamar had helmets. Heald looked like Nero.

Spencer had first crack at the dialogue and brought in Fletcher, whom, in spite of recent experiences, he said he was glad to see.

'You're very well placed there, Commander; orchestra pit you might say. There are some questions we want answers for, and I shall ask you. Lieutenant Kelly here will naturally be too brimming with *esprit de corpse* to tell all; but I'm sure you won't want her to come to harm.'

Tamar said wearily, 'Tell him to go to hell, Dag.'

Spencer struck hard and true at the back of her legs just behind the knees, and she fell forward, unable to save herself, on to the tiled floor. He said equably, 'Unhappily, Ginger, we are following different books of rules.'

It was the last thing said for some time. Dag Fletcher had weakened an area of mesh round a metre square. Concentrating every ounce of strength he could bring to bear, he fairly tore the piece out of the frame and fell through the gap, scratching long parallel grooves from chest to navel on the projecting broken edges.

Vanora was out of luck. She had moved nearer the cage and got the loose piece of grating, with some poetic justice, on the back of her shiny basin. Then she cushioned Dag's fall and when he went forward, seeing only Spencer, through a fine red filter, she stayed down in a small, attractive heap, with a neat waffle pattern on her bare shoulders.

Vernon Spencer had no thought except for the morrow and could see that it was becoming doubtful whether it would dawn for him. He said urgently, 'This is it, Brad. He has to go. Put a bodkin hole in him.' Then he was too busy for much speech. A quick learner, he avoided the grip which had stopped him before and managed to raise a long weal on Dag's neck with his rod.

But Fletcher was well beyond feeling pain. He was also very conscious that his time must be running out and a decision had to be forced. Without noticing that Spencer's other fist was beating into his face, he concentrated on the wrist of the stick hand and seized it, two handed. When the forearm broke the man was already falling, blacked out under extreme pain. He let him go and spun round to see Heald taking deliberate care to prepare his service laser for firing.

It was just like the man. He would have been more comfortable if he could have done the log entry and had clearance for this use before he actually had to do it. In fact he was saved the trouble; Dag left Spencer to join the horizontal party and chopped the weapon out of Heald's hand. He also found time to deliver sentence. 'Mutiny, Heald.'

There was not time for more. The room began to fill up. March and Voller with four new Cappodanians appeared in the aperture of the entrance which the others had used. This was a wide opening with a flat ogee arch and appeared to lead to a circular foyer. There was a moment's pause, whilst they took in the salient facts of the confused scene and Dag gathered in Heald's laser and dropped back centre, to where Tamar was trying to stand. Already stiff and cramped, the blow had more or less paralysed her legs below the knee and she could only kneel.

Dag said, 'Get on my back,' and dropped on one knee beside her.

She said, 'Honestly, I'd like to oblige, but. . . .' Before she could finish, he had his shoulder in her diaphragm and was standing, with Tamar dangling down his back like a lay figure. The roving muzzle of the laser tube was discouraging much movement. He backed towards the unused entrance and was almost there when a new thought struck him. 'Heald. Move. Collect in those tin hats. Quick now.' He was lined up with meticulous accuracy on the captain's navel. Heald shambled urgently round the group gathering peascods and came forward with a nesting set.

Tamar said, 'I can hold those, Dag.' He put the top one on his head and allowed her to grip the rest by their rims against her thigh. Then he continued on his way.

Nobody else moved. The Cappodanians were obviously waiting for instructions, looking about with round black expressionless eyes; Heald, now utterly committed, was regretting that he had not been quick enough; Spencer began to sit up. He said thickly, 'Where is the bastard?'

The nearest Cappodanian watching him closely, like an intelligent dog, pointed to the exit.

'Well, that's all right then. He can't get very far through there. It's just a matter of time.'

'They've got the screens,' Voller was helping Spencer to his feet.

'It's all the same. There's no way out through there. Get me Vanora's laser. No bloody arguments this time; just make holes in either or both. But we need more helmets. Quick now, Don, take a nog and don't hang about. There can't be much time left.'

Voller beckoned the nearest Cappodanian and pointed to his head. The man nodded briefly and padded off at a jog trot with Voller following at a faster saunter than was usual with him. It was clear that Spencer was the acknowledged head of the group. Heald said almost deferentially, 'I'll put a temporary fix on that arm, Spencer,' and began cutting away the thin material of the man's shirt.

Vanora rejoined as an active member and showed another facet of her many sided competence.

'Let me do that, Bwadley. I have a medical qualification.' She ran her fingers lightly over the bulged forearm. 'Vewy lucky, Vernon. It's only a simple fwacture. We shall just have to manage without your mewy clap for a few days. Now you're not going to enjoy this. Just sit down a minute.'

Spencer had given himself a cigarette and blew a long plume of smoke into her face. 'All right, you clever wee devil. Don't press your luck. Just use your healing art without any trimmings or Hippocrates will lose one of his star students.'

Even as he was speaking, she had taken his wrist; and then without warning, she had one foot in his armpit for

purchase and gave a quick pull and twist. The arm
straightened and the fracture dovetailed together. Only a
nimble backward leap saved her from the sideswipe of his free
hand.

Even her self-centred nature was shocked into protest.
'Weally, Vernon, I don't understand you at all. *Anybody* else
would be vewy gwateful. All you need now is a splint. But
you can get somebody else to do that for you.'

'Don't give me that. If it didn't suit your book, you
wouldn't have bothered. But whatever the motive, you've
done well.'

Further development of this fugue of gratitude had to remain unscored. The crystal had cleared and the overwhelming influence of its pervasive frequency transmission inhibited
all new mental bonds and left each mind in a state of rest,
set in the pattern of its strongest bonds, which persisted even
under the electrical interference.

Meanwhile Dag Fletcher was pressing on along corridors
which rose as a sloping ramp and were taking him higher in
the building without option of a change of course. Rounding
the fifth corner, with the pattern emerging, he said, 'I'll get
you out of that corset, then you can shift your fat with your
own horse power.'

There was no reply which was unexpected. In normal form,
she would have taken a bite out of his flank. When he put
her down, she lay still, eyes open, but blank, and he knew
that there would be time for a stop. He prised her fingers loose
from their grip on the metal hemispheres and picked one to
fit her. Even in these brisk times, he had to make a pause
and look at her. She was very vulnerable. Someone had pro-
vided fresh water to rinse the platinum precipitate out of her
hair and it was back in deep, springy waves, setting her broad
oval face in a frame of deep colour, so that the skin was pale
by contrast.

Instead of putting the hat on, he fished out his infrangom

file and hacked through the belt. He lifted her to her feet and
arranged her arms round his neck. Then he dropped the white
hemisphere on its thick, silky bed and tapped it in place. Instantly her eyes cleared and she recognised what he had done.
'You are nice, Dag. I wouldn't want to wake up anywhere
else. I'm glad it's you though. A girl who lived here would
be well advised to keep her hat on.'

'Like the girl on the land scooter.'

'What was she at, then?'

'I'm glad you asked that. She was leaving school and her
headmistress asked her what she was going to do next. She
said that, in the *immediate* future, she was going on an extended sight-seeing tour on the back of her boy-friend's
scooter. They would take a tent and camp out in wild, romantic places. The alarmed pedagogue. . . .'

'What's a pedagogue?' she was so close that he had to blow
a swathe of hair away before he could go on.

'This pedagogue asked whether her mother would not
be anxious for her and she replied that she would be quite
safe, because she always kept her crash helmet on.'

'I'll remember that.' Then her voice changed to concern.
'Dag, this is blood. You're covered with it. You must have lost
a lot. There you go, chatting me up to make me feel better
and I'm letting you bleed to death.'

'Later. You can play hospital orderly later. Let's get on.'

'What about these spare bowlers?'

'Bring them along for now. We could use two for Cormac
and Campbell. Where are they, by the way?'

As they went on at a steady jog trot, hand in hand along
wide, rising ramps which were now clearly zig-zagging round
an oblong structure, she said, 'There are whole suites of
rooms in this complex. When I woke up before, I was in a
dormitory place, like a small hospital ward. I didn't see them.
Purdah arrangements. That's Cappodanian pattern, isn't it?
Pretty strict *apartheit*. Anyway, Vanora came to get me out
and we went down a subway and came up into that circular

foyer just off where you were. They could be in any one of a dozen rooms.'

There was a change in direction. A short horizontal corridor took them nearer to the centre of the structure's mass and then the upward trend began again on shorter lengths and with a steeper incline. Tamar said, 'Defensive castle architecture. You fight your way in and then after working at it for an hour or two you find you've fought your way right through and you're on the outside looking in again.'

Whatever the truth of this observation, the next corner took them to face an edge to edge partition, filling the three metre wide corridor with a solid finality which made it clear why there had been no immediate hue and cry.

'It must open or there's no point in this ramp.' Tamar was knocking at the flat grey surface with the rim of a white bowler.

'Above this, there's open air.'

'Of course, there's a skylight.'

Along their route so far, light had come from circular glowing panels set at the corners of the angular spiral. Now the light was overhead from an oval skylight and had the characteristic green tinge of the planet's natural light. It had the effect of greying off much of the colour in Tamar's hair which in fact made her look more, rather than less, youthful.

'You've gone grey in this light. It suits you. You'll make a very distinguished older citizen.'

'However you survived until now is a constant puzzle to me. Less social chat and more finding a way out.'

To be fair, Dag Fletcher had spoken absently, he was already thinking it out with nine tenths of his mind and had used the remainder automatically to head her off the difficulty. Without replying, he began methodically drilling holes in the rim of the skylight. Looking for the catch in the door, if there was one, could easily take much longer and its material sounded rock solid. Fine spoil floated down and added its mite to the blood and sweat texture of his chest. He could have modelled for a disaster victim without a question asked.

Tamar back-tracked two turns of the ramp and put her ear to the ground. All it picked up was dust. They could have been sharing the place with Akhnaten. As that thought struck her, she remembered some data from an ethnology tape on Cappodanian customs. They lived in community style dwellings—a sophistication of the Dyak long house—and had a thing about keeping their dead in the house. The blind building could be to do with that. Probably the long, rising ramp symbolised something. Then the closed door. By and large, it might have been just as well that they had not gone through it. She tried the floor again. Without being absolutely sure, there could be a recurrent scuff from well below. Back to the coal face then.

Seeing him fresh, in the shaft of green light from above was a *memento mori* in itself. She said, 'Dag, this could be a sepulchre full of the sheeted dead, they won't mind you; but they'll notice me, I hope.'

Not being privileged to follow the full score, this *coda* seemed to him to be pure gibberish. He said, 'Up on my back and push like hell.'

As the mounting buckled aside, she remembered the main issue. 'They're on the way up. About four floors down.' Then she was pulling herself into the green light of Thirza's day. Dag jumped for the grip and then hauled himself through. They stood on a twenty metre square platform which fell away without parapet or rail to a larger square fifteen metres below. Its centre was dominated by a large oval dome rising above the general level to a good three metres at its apex.

Dag twisted their manhole cover back into place. Any new arrival would be held up by it long enough to win himself a hole in the head.

There was a good deal to see. The top of the ziggurat put them level with the first fold of rising ground beyond the lake and the culture pattern of the residents was laid out for them like a text book illustration. The village itself was one integral structure with rambling additions thrown out to meet increasing needs. Walled on the lakeside to protect it from the rising water. Backing into the hill so that some parts of it were virtually subterranean.

Tamar said, 'Terracing, Dag. Looks like quite advanced hydroponics, there isn't much soil. Fed from tanks cut into the rock. No animal life though. Must be a vegetarian diet.'

'Not necessarily. Those tanks could be for fish. If the ancestors of these people came in a ship, they would have fish embryos in the survival bank.'

'That 'diet' is a loaded word. Do we get to eat?'

Fletcher was leaning over the centre dome to look down into the building. In the dim green light, which fell like a shaft into confusing distance, there appeared to be a regular pattern of lines and rings round spiralling gallery walls. Circling, until he could look at the point where the blocked door lay, he saw that the spiral ended there in a square landing like a reception area, with a toast rack of white metal just inside. One thing was clear enough, it would have been a waste of time to work on the door. Its inner surface was rough ceramic block. Tamar was probably right then. It was some kind of vault, broken open for each visit and sealed again as if for ever.

Tamar called, 'They're here,' and even as he turned away, the train of thought had brought the pattern into perspective, the lines and rings were erect human figures. Round faced, Cappodanian dead lining the walls in patient expectation. Well, they would not mind waiting a little longer.

The lid was going up in a tentative way. Dag squatted on his heels, a metre from its rising edge. A section of rod showed, then another and a united push sent the flap back. Tamar joined him and they watched the hole, like bizarre eskimos waiting for a seal. Spencer's voice, muffled but authoritative, was telling Voller to get his finger out and lift a nog up to take a look.

When a round dome appeared, Fletcher had already made up his mind. The Cappodanians had acquiesced in their imprisonment and were clearly sold on the Vanora party line, whatever that was. If consequences followed which were not all pleasing, they had only themselves to blame. He bored the little fatal hole with judicial accuracy in the centre of the brim. The man fell back, a mute but eloquent fifth column, spreading discouragement.

One immediate outcome was a high keening wail from the rest of the party. Seconds later it was taken up from all parts of the building and Spencer's voice could only just be heard saying, 'Never mind, Vanora, let them go. It hardly matters. We've got Fletcher up a tree and they'll be more than ever convinced that he's no good for them. It couldn't have happened better. We'll follow them down. Not you, Voller. You stay. You saw what happened; you know what to do with anyone coming through the roof?'

'Kelly too?'

'Yes, don't get sentimental. With the kind of money you are going to have you can buy a dozen like that. All right?'

'If you say so.'

'I do say so. Come along, Vanora. Don't walk behind me like a squaw.'

The wailing stopped, having passed its message to all interested parties. Tamar said, 'Should you have done that?'

'Yes.'

He went back to the centre dome and began etching out a trap door. When it was perforated all round, he gave it a smart tap and the piece fell through, a stone dropping down a well. A gust of heavily aromatic air wafted out.

'It smells like ripe bananas.' Then she saw why. 'Dag, you're surely not taking me down there?'

'Yes.' Once again the flat monosyllable and she realised that he was in a phase which she had not seen before. He had withdrawn into a concentration of purpose almost as absolute as the mind-bending effect of the crystal. When he met her eyes, she knew that he was not seeing her in the terms of their intimate relationship. For now, she was just a useful agent in some design exterior to them both.

She said, 'How do we miss dropping down the middle?'

He was already stripping off his tough thin slacks and the remnants of his shirt. Ripped in broad strips and knotted into lengths, he had two four metre ragged ropes.

'Not enough?'

'No.'

'Since you can hardly have set up anything as elaborate as this with a simple ulterior motive, you shall have my all.'

'Make it quick.'

When he had three lengths he said, 'Sennet, very strong. Hold the ends.' Then he plaited the three strands into one chunky rope. When it was finished, there were three metres. It hung down into the well with its free end a metre out from the line of the nearest platform and four metres above it. Then he came out of his preoccupation long enough to put hands on her bare shoulders and say, 'My only worry is that you'll get them all moving down there. You look more beautiful than any human being has any right to be. I'll go first and beat off the rush.'

He was lowering himself through the gap, deeply browned, slim but powerfully muscled, looking more compact and athletic in short briefs than his usual loose-limbed relaxed gait would suggest.

At the end of the rope, he was still short of the target and began to swing. When the pendulum motion took him over the landing, he timed it to the split second and dropped like a cat.

'Your turn.'

A doubtful Eurydice, Tamar Kelly went cautiously through the gap. When she was almost at the end, his guiding hands were reaching up to the seat of her black and frivolous pants.

'Let go.'

It was a triumph of faith—that willingness to accept the noblest hypothesis—which made her reaction instantaneous.

He gathered her in and they stood together in the dim green light, watched by the incurious dead. The colour had drained out of her hair and it was grey silk falling like a personal acoustic cowl onto his chest until he put back her head and kissed her lips. They were soft and cool and slightly tremulous.

'Dag?'

'Here, present.'

'These people were once like us.'

'Nobody has ever been like you.'

'You know what I mean.'

'I do and this is not the time to go into it. You know this is your last mission?'

'Is it?'

'Yes. When we get back, you marry me and stay put. Don't say anything. There isn't anything to say. That's it. Final. Now we move on.'

They went down the long ramp hand in hand into gathering green darkness.

CHAPTER EIGHT

'THAT'S odd.'

'Your curiosity never sleeps. What is it then?'

They were well down inside the mausoleum and she was walking on the outside, preferring the long drop to the silent witnesses.

'They're mainly men.'

She might equally have said that they all looked very cheerful, considering the state they were in. Faces had been set in the lines of a smiling mask. But it was fair comment. The unclothed figures in their niches were uniformly well equipped to preserve the species, and the embalmers had tended to make a feature of the fact. A more obvious vanity than display usually is. Only every tenth or so was female; short stocky, prototypes of the *Venus naturalis*; fertility figurines.

'Polyandrous society. Historically it was so on Cappodan. They revived the idea. If the first settlers were from a ship it would naturally fall out that way. Not a stable system, I should think. Decanters surrounding a glass instead of glasses round a decanter.'

'You're a "glasses round a decanter" man?'

'No, I just brought that in because I thought of it. Individual values can only be maintained on a one to one basis. Think of all the communities you know. Which are the most stable?'

'Keep talking. I don't want to find myself signed up as seventh slave of the bedchamber.'

The figures stopped abruptly and empty niches lined the

inner wall. It saved him a reply. They must be getting down now to their starting point. He went on a different tack. 'One thing is sure. They've been living here for several centuries. It can't be a big group. This lot must represent twenty generations.'

'Uzziah begat Jotham and Jotham begat Ahaz and all that jazz?'

'And we must be getting on.'

'You do shine in a tomb, Dag. I'll know where to take you on a wet day.' Then she was suddenly serious, looking back the way they had come. 'We could be standing like that, side by side, and you wouldn't know I was there.'

'Don't be too sure about that.'

'You haven't got anything of mine, have you? Take this ring,' she was twisting a small electrum signet ring from her little finger.

'Can you spare it? You haven't got much else on?'

Then he saw she was serious and took it in the same spirit. 'I haven't anything to give you. You'll have to wait.'

'For as long as forever is.'

'I should be able to manage something before then.'

He went back to the last figure in the row. Thin lines of something like catgut held the smiling cadaver from falling forward on to the passer by. He snapped off a half metre length and rejoined her, looping the ring like a crucifix round his neck.

They had gone on another seven paces before the Cappodanian made a bid to get his string back. It had been a clever cat's cradle with a continuous piece, and it now unwove from the shackle, allowing him to lean out and pass his point of no return. He was a well rounded little man and began to roll down the ramp after them. But lacking much sense of direction he missed the corner turn and overbalanced into the well.

Tamar, glancing round, saw his disappearing heels. 'Oh my God, Dag. You've done it now. Look.'

The thin cord had been continuous even further back. A symbolic link, uniting the residents in an unbroken thread of democratic cohesion. Resurrect one, resurrect all. Number two was already on the way with the next in line leaning out.

'Dag, it's ghastly. It wouldn't be so bad if they weren't grinning about it.'

'Don't look. They can't get round the bend.'

Now they were two spirals below and every minute a new diver took his plunge down the well.

'Any going round the bend will be done by me.' There was a note of real terror in her husky voice and he transferred his hold to where a nubile hip moved companionably under his hand.

Two more circuits and he estimated they were level with their outside starting point. He had to lean out and look up at the distant skylight to decide which side they ought to be. The dead were still coming down, isochronous as the beat of a flail.

It was the other side and they went down again to get there. Then he looked at the wall.

'Take a niche while you're waiting.'

'Thank you very much. I'll just watch you work.'

But in the event, it was Tamar who found the way. He had started drilling fine laser holes in the back of an alcove, hoping to peel off a section of the smooth rendering and take a look at the structure beneath, she had nerved herself to go further on, down the gloomy ramp, trying to close her ears and mind to the noises of the jolly divers.

'Dag.'

'What is it?'

'There's a change here. This is where the building starts. The rest is excavation.'

'I can't hear you.'

'Well come here.'

'I hope this is worth while.'

He joined her and for a moment she was sidetracked into wanting to bang his head on the rock. She settled for, 'That's typical. Look.' She pulled at the rock face where its surface was unevenly ridged and it broke away like dark cake.

'We can dig a way out.'

'You couldn't tunnel in that, it would crumble in.'

'Just below the building line so that the masonry floor is a roof.'

'Sorry. I'm being stupid. You're right of course.'

She was already using a spare hat as a scoop and throwing the spoil into the busy shaft. Together, making alternate scrapes at the coal face they began to show progress. The pediment of the wall went back a metre, then they followed it up, lying on the gritty porous rock, for another two. When they hit stone again. Tamar lay down in the evil darkness. Although he could not see her, he knew she was crying silently.

'Sorry, Dag. I can't do any more just now. Perhaps we should have gone the way you were going.'

'No, this was the right decision.'

She needed comfort. He could not imagine a more incongruous place for her vivid person to be, literally blacked out and the only personality clue left, her warm husky voice.

'Tamar, I'd rather be here with you than anywhere else with anybody at all.' Then their hands were eyes in their narrow grave, refuting Donne's maxim that 'none I think do there embrace', recreating each, the other, in fond detail.

She said, 'It's really very lucky. We've both got crash hats on.'

*　　*　　*

Vanora, in the pose of Uli Nimptsch's *Olympia*, was looking at Vernon Spencer with an impatience which gathered from many levels. At the most obvious, she was not used to being looked at with indifference even by anyone handicapped in the matter of having one arm in a restricting splint. She was sitting on one of the thick reclining mats much used by the Cappodanians, left arm falling straight below its shoulder, forearm along the mat, tapering to a pointing index finger which she was beginning to tap, right arm, a narrow angled buttress behind her, with palm flat and fingers spread. Her right leg was extended straight out and crossed over the left which was drawn up and tucked underneath, so that the neat sole of a foot appeared, as if disembodied, beside her right knee.

It was a pose which emphasised an unexpected generosity in the curve of her hip and tautened every pectoral muscle in the charts.

Spencer was saying, 'You should really think things out better than this, Vanora. You ought to have known about the radio blanket on Thirza. Have you any idea at all what power you would need to belt a signal through?'

She might well have replied that in some directions it appeared unlikely that a signal would ever get through; but she kept to the point with, 'You know the power Fletcher could use. There's nothing in the car to wesemble that.'

'What about the crystal?'

'What about it then? It has the good taste to appweciate my vital statistics, but when you've said that you've said all. It exists to gwow and to contemplate its navel as far as one can tell.'

'There again you miss a great point. It has this planet organised for itself and indirectly for us. We shall have to use it.'

'How so?'

'It's developed those tubular syphons to bring in alluvial sludge from every shore to this complex of lakes. At first the fact that the next lake flushed down into this one as soon as it reached a certain level must have been a useful accident; but it now controls the operation to an exact schedule.'

'So?'

'It's a great gift to any platinum extraction operation. Everything is concentrated here. One centre. It does nine tenths of the job. These nogs saw that and pitched their tent here. I suppose the first lot thought they'd have it made when a relief ship came. When it didn't, they just went on working at it, as a way of life. There must be thousands of tons of platinum so far, stock piled, from gleanings on the beach, and the crater itself is full of it.'

'When then?'

'Details don't matter at this stage; but your employers can work something out which keeps the crystal working and rakes in a percentage. Then when the lake begins to drop you have the final reserve of the thing itself, a mountain of the metal. Meanwhile, to revert to the here and now. Can't you canalise the energy there into a signal to talk to your frigate? Bring her down here. They'll have to eliminate these nogs or I.G.O. will have a clear right of colonisation to annex the planet.'

'That's my Vernon. Use the cwystal, then destwoy it. Wipe out the sad little men. But you're quite wight. I'm only surpwised you didn't mention Fletcher.'

'He's fixed anyway. He can't leave that roof. *Interstellar X* won't get far on the skeleton crew it has. Voller will be useful, but I think Heald and Marsh should join the nogs.'

'All wight, Vernon. I'll do it your way.' She seemed suddenly resigned to a purely business conference and sat forward, drawing up both knees and clasping her hands round them. 'And I *have* been thinking about using that cwystal. It twansmits at a low level on a wide fwont. Make it twansmit on a narrow fwont at a high level.'

'You'll talk to it?'

'Indiwectly, yes. But Bwuce Marsh can help. He'll know how to engineer this. I want all the scweening matewial that can be assembled awanged in a pawaboloidal curve along the shore.'

'How long is this going to take?'

'Do be weasonable, Vernon. We don't even know whether it will work at all, do we? It depends on how quickly you can organise the matewials. Incidentally, I don't think that nice boy Campbell knows anything about his ship's pwogwamme, so you can save time by not bothewing him any more. Cormac will never speak. Venusians just don't understand about pain. It doesn't wowy them.'

Spencer, more saturnine than normal, with the beginnings of a black beard and a pallor accentuated by the green light. looked at her speculatively.

'You're too clever by half, Vanora. When it's set up, I'll talk to the frigate. A precocious little bleeder like yourself might put the wrong emphasis on affairs. Who are they up there?'

'You still don't twust me, Vernon.'

'Who are they?'

'Scotians, I think. That would be the neawest gwoup for O.G.A. to use on this mission.'

'Scotia, the dark planet. I hope you know what you're doing. They're barely human. That's why they're in O.G.A. The planet was on the proscribed list "a community of such opposed principles that it could not be assimilated and would be a threat to established systems".'

'It should suit you vewy well.'

'But then I am not a small, lush looking female. You'll be lucky to see Scotia alive.'

'You're twying to fwighten me, I have diplomatic immunity.'

'Well, you'd better keep your badge in your hand and wave it constantly about or it won't be noticed.' He was looking more cheerful at her discomfiture. 'Or you can cut your hair and sew yourself into a thick sack and make like an assiduous cabin boy.'

He went out to get Marsh busy and Vanora stood up, almost as still as one of her statues. In spite of the casual malice in Spencer's remarks, there was some truth there. She had overlooked that aspect, being so sure of her official rank at the O.G.A. Central Office. But would they be greatly concerned on her account? Certainly not to the extent of provoking an incident with Scotia. Agents were on their own in the field and could not expect support even when a mission was successfully completed; even when the danger was from their own side. Damn Spencer for being right. She had planned to ditch him when his usefulness was done; but now it seemed that he was necessary for longer. He could speak to the Scotians and take her along under protection. But she could wait. Once in the O.G.A. consulate on Scotia it would be a different matter.

* * *

Time no longer meant anything, exhaustion meant nothing. Even the nearness of the other toiling body meant nothing. When a finger of green light exploded down into their black burrow, Tamar could only carry on with the routine chore of passing back the hatful of crumbling black shale.

Dag Fletcher squeezed past her and cautiously enlarged the small gap. They had made a horizontal run of five more metres, in choking grime, to the edge of the masonry floor above. Then they had turned up beside it and into the light of Thirza's day. When he pushed out his grimy, miner's head, he saw that they were on the outside of the building between it and the sea wall. The flooring above was a pavement strip which surrounded the walls like a flange.

Nobody was in sight; but as his ears came out of the burrow, he picked up noises from the foreshore. The little people were working over the wall. He lifted out a ragged ball of shale and then heaved himself over the flaky rim, careful not to cave the funnel on to his cell mate. Then he leaned back in and patted her round hat, which by some grime-repelling property had alone remained reasonably clean.

'What are you doing in that hole?'

'I don't know that I could force myself to marry a man with such a short memory. I'm waiting to take a bite out of any passing leg.'

It was a point. They could not go on much longer without food. They lay in the warm green light, grateful for a stop in the killing labour and grateful for the oxygen-rich air. Fletcher looked around. They were a third of the way along the complex. Fifty metres towards the centre of the curving wall was a gateway. The scout car must be somewhere. Probably in the central courtyard. That in fact would be the best find. Food, clothes and its equalising force of fire power.

'Come on.'

She stood up obediently, still carrying the spare hats like begging bowls. She even managed, 'All we need is a barrel organ.'

Still no one came. Moving silently along the pavement they reached the archway and he motioned to her to flatten against the wall. Then he edged along to the supporting shaft of the arch and looked round. The opening tunnelled into a thickness of building like a gatehouse and led into a clearing. It was empty as far as could be seen.

They went on, black shadows against the off-white walls. The inner yard was a long ellipse and the scout car was down left close to an archway and a line of window openings. Dag said, 'Stay here,' and was moving before she could reply.

Tamar Kelly after being as close to him as she could well get, felt suddenly that she had been deserted at the altar. The archway was now a lonely place and she was conscious that her clothing, once minimal, was now negligible. No prude and much travelled in cultures like Vanora's where nudity was an unconsidered thing, she still could not avoid feeling especially vulnerable. Fortunately, there was something to watch which took her mind off herself.

Dag had reached the car and she saw him try to slide back the canopy door. It was obviously locked. Heald no doubt had a careful streak and would have locked up even to take a walk round a deserted asteroid. He was carefully drilling out the mechanism with a laser beam when Heald himself appeared in the open arch. She had opened her mouth to shout when Fletcher saw the man for himself and simply swivelled the beam to hit his ex-Co-pilot between the eyes.

Seen from a distance it looked like a callous mime, and Tamar felt suddenly chilled by the finality of it. Heald fell sideways, until he was leaning on an invisible wall and then began to slide down it, a sack of inanimate matter, settling to a stable level. By the time he had found his equilibrium Dag had completed his locksmith's chore and the door was sliding back. Seconds later, the car was sidling towards her at zero thrust, with the door still open, and when Dag's arm round her shoulders helped her in, it was like getting back into bed on a chilly night.

'What about the others?'

'Later. We can't do much good just now. Drop over the ridge and sort ourselves out.'

He was lifting the car in vertical ascent to clear the buildings, when they heard the wail for a death being taken up from wherever there were Cappodanians. Someone had found Heald. The embalmers would have a field day with that portly figure. What would happen when they opened the vault to put the two new boys in was a sobering thought. Cultures were touchy on matters of funerary custom. It could well spark off a crisis in public relations.

Food there still was in an unopened emergency pack—a standard fitting in the patrol car. She fed him a strip of concentrate. 'Have this to be going on with. There's fresh water too. How long will we be?'

'Minutes only. I can wait. What's the time?'

'Ten past fugit.'

'Come again.'

'1610.'

'So, there isn't long before Charlton takes the ship up. I gave him four days. If he goes up now, that frigate will have him on a plate. It looks as though we should split up. You to circle round and pick up the trolley. Go straight back and tell all. He can wait another two days. I want to have a look for Campbell and Cormac.'

For a moment, she was unable to speak, then she said very huskily, 'Please let me stay with you, Dag. It'll not make much difference time-wise. If you can get them out we'd still be in good time to warn Charlton.'

It was the first time she had ever appealed to him on a personal level to influence a decision. He realised that after the last three days and in particular the last twenty-four hours, she would not feel like a tough trek round the lake and a lonely slog back over the tundra. Even then, it was unusual. It was not the thought of hardship, of course; she simply didn't want to leave him. He, himself, for his own self's sake because she wanted to be with him. His hesitation had been long enough for her to sense his dilemma and she went on. 'All right. Don't worry. Sorry, Dag. Of course, I'll go.'

But having reached the point in his deliberations when the thought of her love had added its weight as a real issue, he knew he could not send her on that journey. Against judgement he said, 'No, you're right. It won't take long. One way or the other, we'll know soon after dark, and the car can take us back in a fraction of the time we took in the trolley. I'll trouble you for another sliver of that concentrate and then a cigarette, if there are any.'

He got both, with a bonus of warm lips brushing the back of his neck. Then he was putting the car neatly on a smooth slab, which tongued out into a water terrace, out of sight of the crater lake and its settlement; a mere fold in the side of the hill, a hundred metres long and twenty metres wide, with clear fresh water at a uniform depth of a metre and a half.

Tamar had dived in from the step and was forging up the pool in an Olympic crawl, before he had dug himself out from behind the console. He first stood on the car's roof and quartered the horizon, satisfying himself that there was no one near enough to reach them before he could reach the controls. Nothing moved. He reckoned that anyone crossing any horizon, as of now, would take more than five minutes to get to the car. He took a short run along the roof and went in after her.

Amongst its bric-a-bac of stores in the narrow locker, the car carried two lightweight atmosphere suits as a reconnaissance facility if it took its crew into a region of bad air. Designed on similar lines to the full space gear, they had detachable linings.

When Tamar finally swam back to the rock, Dag had an inner suit laid out for her with a strip of cloth for a towel and a tin of plain talc.

'Dag. You must be the most thoughtful Commander in the service.' She was standing with her back to him drying her hair, an Ingres figure.

He said, 'A man could take a lifetime painting you like that and think it well spent.'

'But whilst his lifetime was living itself out, I should be growing old and he wouldn't want to paint me then.'

'You're too practical. You should take these theoretical compliments strictly at surface level.'

'Just insincere flattery. It will get you nowhere.'

A line of verse from way back swam into mind, like a reluctant fish, bringing no context. 'With longings shaped like naked girls, they dream,' something about voyagers. There could be no juster image of that state of mind, which, as a traveller, he knew well. And Tamar completed the unsatisfied equations, making an end of galactic wandering a feasible thing. He could make this his last mission and hook himself to a desk. Then he realised with some bitterness that it was a conclusion which he had arrived at a bit late in the day. There was almost no chance at all, the way things were falling out, that any of them would get back.

When Tamar stopped her brisk towelling and ran quickly to him to kneel beside him and claim the cigarette he was smoking, he was already thinking out the next move and his question was as removed from her mood as it could well be.

'Did you see Heald or any of the others when you came up from your *zenana*?'

She was disappointed that the small idyll was over. But she knew it was just. She kept the cigarette and climbed into her suit.

'Heald joined us. I think he came out of one of the rooms off that circular hall.'

'There would be others like the one I was in. They'd be kept handy. No doubt they've been questioned.'

Suddenly she was contrite, 'I'm being selfish. They might be badly hurt. If you want me to go on, I will.'

'No, that's settled. Dark in under the hour. Not that it makes a lot of difference, because the lights are always burning on the lake; but getting away will be easier. I'd like to know roughly where they are.'

'Ask somebody.'

She was ready. Suit legs turned in to a trim length and sleeves rolled up, a white head band improvised from the first-aid kit. 'Yes, we'll do that now. There must be some honest toilers at work on the farm. Let's take a look.'

Two brown Cappodanians, knee deep in a rice paddy, looked at the car with round eyes. Their ancestors had waited with diminishing hope for the arrival of a relief ship. Now that the long seclusion had been broken, nobody seemed to know how to treat the visitors, or indeed whether they represented total good or not. Vanora, anyway, had probably sold them the idea that she represented the official party and anyone else was to be distrusted.

Tamar jumped down and stood with them as a democratic gesture and the first sign of animation appeared. Even in the green light her hair was startling enough, and when one pointed at it and began to jabber excitedly, she sensed that hostility was on the wane. In fact it was an even bet whether or not she got a joint proposal on the spot. As a communications executive, she had fluent command of the major language groups of the galaxy and a simplified *lingua franca* which was intelligible almost everywhere. Speaking slowly, she asked if they knew about the other travellers.

At first, they concentrated on Vanora. It was clear that the men of the planet had more thorough going one-track minds than most. Given the green gloom and the scenery, it was probably inevitable. Then she moved them on. Yes, there were others. A fat man—Heald—they didn't know that he was no longer in service. A thin tall man and a man with a broken arm, who was always with the woman. Here they wanted to digress again about Vanora. It took time, but Tamar finally got round to it. Two men were being kept in a cell. An old man and a young one. Where? There was a holding room off the main dining place. So that they would always be under supervision. They seemed quite ingenuous. The point of the questioning was not apparent to them. Tamar finally went beyond her brief and invited them in as guides.

They sat in the rear seats, very erect, looking round the interior of the small car and talking in fast undertones, which she could not follow. Dag said, 'We'll go over the complex. Get them to identify the buildings. Pin-point this dining place, put an orientated sketch on the navigation panel, then we can find it in the dark.'

'It never is dark.'

'It will be.'

She asked no more questions and they dropped over the lip of the ridge and Tamar was working with deft precise movements of the stylus to knock out a copy of the layout ahead on to the grid lines of the car's miniature presentation table.

The two men watched her with open admiration and responded eagerly to every question. They seemed to be anxious to make a good impression. Dag lined up on the axis of the elliptical complex and came in on a convenient North/South bearing. It could not have been simpler to set up for automatic navigation. He took them just above roof level of the highest building, and they had a clear view of the platform which they had stood on. It was empty but the two broken skylights were clear to see and the two passengers became very excited. Then they were over the courtyard and Tamar had her work cut out to get them to concentrate long enough to point out the main features.

'It's done.'

'Back to the hills then. I'll drop them further up, so that they can't get back before we want to act.'

'That doesn't seem very kind when they've been so helpful.'

'Just because they want to join your family group. Ask them where everybody is just now.'

Dag turned out beyond the lakeside wall in his sweep back and the question was superfluous. The narrow beach was an ant hill of activity. In the centre, Vanora and Spencer were watching the operation, like staff officers on a knoll. Marsh was clearly bearing the brunt of the day, limping about directing the labour force, Voller was not immediately visible, but could be taking a break in some backwater out of Vanora's sight. Whatever they were building had now reached near completion in the form of a long curve with recognisable mathematical properties.

Dag said, 'What would they want a parabola for?'

It was immediately plain to his communications executive. 'It's a big reflector or concentrator. Of course, concentrator. They're going to use the output of the crystal to punch out a signal. Communicate with the frigate.'

Time was shrinking for them. But in one way the situation was better. Dag was already turning into the courtyard. 'We'll get them out now. There can't be many left inside. Tell your friends to take me to where the prisoners are. When we leave, take the car up to ten metres and blast anybody who tries to get through that arch.'

Then he was down and opening the door, whilst she went at it in husky, persuasive tones with gestures that would have won her a place in an oriental school of mime. When they finally climbed out, they were looking apprehensively at the tall block of the spiral vault and seemed reluctant to go away from it. A burst of jabbering from one seemed to settle a point. They went at a trot through the entrance where Heald had stood and Fletcher followed.

Tamar, feeling suddenly deserted, took up a sentry post in the centre, swivelling slowly, with her fingers lightly on the firing bar of the multitube laser which lay along the axis of the car. She switched in the monitor, although it had been useless so far in the conditions of electrical screening. Even communication to the corvette was impossible. She felt to some extent guilty about that. Surely there was something she could have done? But the answer, if there was one, did not come. So she thought about Dag and wondered whether she was ready to leave the service.

Dag Fletcher found himself in the corridor behind the arch with his two guides already getting ahead. He had made up the distance, when they stopped together and pointed him on through a further arch on the right leading into the mass of the building. He motioned them to go through, but for the first time there was resistance. As if on a signal they ran further along the corridor and dodged into the next opening.

It would have been just possible to drop one or both of them before they disappeared, but whatever gain that would make would have been marginal. He went instead through the nearer arch and found that it was indeed a dining space. Long low tables ran from end to end, seating for possibly three hundred people. He was about central. Far right there was a food preparation area and a number of women in yellow smocks were busy putting out flat circles of dark brown bread on trays. Far left was a long familiar grille with a cell behind it at waist level. This time any occupants were on view and it dawned suddenly on him that the set-up gave the lie to any appearance of benevolent charm the inhabitants might have. It was designed to allow the prisoner to starve in the sight of plenty and make a Roman holiday for the diners.

Cormac was standing, leaning on the back wall, dour and craggy as ever. He had been given a screening hat so that he could remain fully conscious of the pleasures of the situation. Campbell was not in sight.

The women made no move to stop him, but as he went down between the tables to the grille, he saw one move quickly out as though she was off to fetch a gendarme. Then he had snapped back the fastening and was helping Cormac through. Campbell had taken off his hat and was lying on his back on a litter of straw bedding. When Dag pushed it in place and helped him up he could hardly stand.

Cormac said, 'They tried to make him answer some questions, but he would not. He is a very worthy young man.'

Between them they helped him out and started down the aisle with him in the middle. Dag left them at the arch and went to the watching cooks. He took a jug of water and two loaves.

'Wait a minute or two. We have time.'

When they were ready to go there was movement at the buttery hatch. Three Cappodanian men appeared and one was in a robe of office and carried a short staff. Cormac said, 'He is their headman. Vanora has persuaded him that she represents O.G.A. and has arranged an alliance.'

Dag Fletcher made the formal announcement which he had used on so many routine landfalls. It might do no good, but it could do no harm.

'Commander Fletcher of the I.G.O. corvette *Interstellar X*. I charge you to give all help in your power to my mission. Do not interfere now.'

He had his laser aligned in the centre of the man's chest and they came no further. Nor did the headman make any reply. They watched in silence as Dag resumed his journey and went out of sight through the arch.

CHAPTER NINE

WHEN Vanora's signal punched itself out, with enough power to run a region for a week, the effect on the car's monitor was dramatic. It virtually shouted its message down Tamar's ear and she involuntarily tightened her grip on the firing bar. A furrow tore itself along the centre of the pavement under the archway and brought utter discouragement to a group of Cappodanians who had been hesitating about approaching the hovering car.

She adjusted the level with rapid economical movements and began to get the gist of it. At first, the language seemed so way out that it meant nothing. Then she realised it was outside the usual groups and needed a different logic. Vanora was speaking in clear incisive phrases from the Esperanto form used by O.G.A., but it was slanted towards Scotian, she must be talking to a ship from the dark planet. It was a one-way message; because they could not reply and she was instructing the commander, as by right of senior rank in the area, to bring down his ship as near the complex as he could get. She was signing off when Dag appeared from the building.

Tamar carved another furrow under the arch and then edged the car back and dropped it neatly beside the three. Campbell was looking better for the food and the resurge of optimism about a possible future. But he still looked bad enough to bring out the latent Florence Nightingale, and she was a minute or two helping him in before she gave Dag the recent news.

'Scotians. That's a different thing again. They're only marginally allied to O.G.A. Vanora can't know what she's doing. She's signed her own death warrant for one thing and everybody else's as well.'

Even Cormac was moved out of his habitual calm. 'This is serious, Commander. There have been many resolutions that Scotia should be destroyed; always defeated by chairborne administrators who had no personal knowledge of that people. It is useless to speak of agreements or usage or international law to them. These concepts are meaningless. They are totally amoral and naturally vicious. It surprises me that they can co-operate with one another well enough to operate a team venture like a space ship. We must withdraw and seek help from a full squadron.'

'That is not easy to do with the frigate waiting for us. We have very little freedom of action left. No time was mentioned, Tamar?'

'None. Work it out from now. If the commander up there takes any notice of Vanora, he should begin to move at once.'

'How long would it take you to work out a landfall from a parking orbit?'

'It depends on local conditions. This was straightforward. Ten minutes give or take another five.'

'Then perhaps two orbital paths to get the ship lined up on your plot?'

'From where they are, certainly not more than two.'

'That means they can be down here in three hours.'

'Yes.'

'It's the break we need. We can be moving the second they touch down and we'll have them cold.'

Cormac said, 'It is an act of war. But you have no choice.'

'Now we know they are Scotians I am only surprised that they have not attacked before now.'

'It suggests that they are part of a larger force. As far as we are concerned, that can make no difference.'

Tamar said, 'I feel sorry for the Cappodanians. Shouldn't you try to warn them, Dag?'

He was back in the driving seat and they were ready to go.

'Rig the outside speaker, I'll hover over the beach and you can tell them the tale.'

Cormac began, 'Commander, I must. . . .' Then he met Tamar's eye and stopped. When he went on he had clearly altered what was originally intended, 'I hope you will make it brief. Our first duty, after all, is to this mission and not to people who have chosen to bring trouble on to themselves.'

A crowd of fifty or more of the little men were moving about uncertainly in front of the gatehouse entrance to the courtyard, spreading back to the wall, where a moving section had been run aside to give access to the beach. There, more had gathered and were waiting to take their turn to go through. It was a picture of day's end at the co-operative. Honest toilers downing tools for the night. Vanora and Spencer were still in the centre of the long parabola. Marsh and Voller were looping in a long length of shining wire which led from a portable transmitter sited against the wall.

All stopped whatever they were at and watched the car. Dag took it slowly to a central point not twenty metres from Vanora and nodded to Tamar to tell the tale.

It was very well done. Whatever the impact of Vanora's personality, she could not match the quality of Tamar's earnest, husky voice in selling an honest line. It conveyed absolute sincerity and its effect was plain even on Marsh and Voller. She called the Cappodanians to remember their ancient heritage and their traditional loyalty to the I.G.O. alliance. She promised in the name of the I.G.O. commissar that any act up to now would be overlooked, if they would resume allegiance to this group of which their mother planet was still a respected and influential member. Then she frankly stated that the present mission was to estimate the mineral wealth of Thirza and that it had not been suspected that it was inhabited. Since however they were in possession, they would be treated as *de facto* owners of the great wealth and would be given treaty rights to a substantial share of it. This was very much better than merely having it with nothing to buy with it. Silver has no colour unless it shine with moderate use. A classical touch which pleased Cormac and got an approving nod.

Volume was high enough for the speech to be heard from one end of the beach to the other. Vanora saw its effect but was powerless to stop the transmission. She tried.

'Vernon. Can't you weach them from here? Dwill a little hole in that wed girl?'

It was extreme range for any accuracy with the small laser and using it left handed was a great handicap. But he steadied his arm on Vanora's head and was ready to do his best when Dag turned the car to bring both of them in direct line of the underslung tubes. It was such an obvious gesture, that he took the hint and stuffed the small weapon back into his belt.

Tamar had now left the theme of obligation and was more definitely plugging the issue of self interest. She pointed out that the Scotian ship, which had been invited in, contained people who would not respect any law or contract whatsoever. The likely outcome was that the Cappodanians would be destroyed to a man as inconvenient witnesses of prior possession. This was obviously a more telling point than any yet.

When she stopped, Cormac said, 'You would make a great diplomat, Lieutenant Kelly. You should join my branch of the service. I think they are ready to listen to what you want them to do.'

He could have been right. The little men were coming forward to stand below the car, making gestures of goodwill, turning their backs symbolically on Vanora. But there was an aural intervention which first stopped them in their tracks and then a physical one in the shape of the headman no less, which set back the clock to pre-Kelly-oration time and indeed injected a whole new feature of positive hostility.

The wail for the dead, with an urgent clamour more striking than any yet, sounded from the depths of the building. Then the headman in a screaming treble, shaking with anger and fear was stabbing his staff of office towards the car and telling a tale which only gave simple pleasure to Spencer.

Tamar said, 'Those men we took as guides saw the roof. They've been to check. They'll know about the muddle in there. They don't like it.'

The headman's address was a classic demonstration that although an audience can be convinced by a good speaker with an honest brief, it can be more easily moved to action by hysterical repetition of some emotive thing. Care for the dead had been elevated to the rank of religious observance. Although Tamar's linguistic skill did not take her every step of the way, she picked up enough to know that 'sacrilege' was being claimed and the only full and perfect oblation would be found in the death of those concerned.

It was a bitter reversal for the fledgling orator. Pride in achievement had made her feel that perhaps Cormac was right and she had seen herself giving her time to politics when she left the service. Dag coming home from the office would find a note on the clock. 'Darling. Back 2130 hours. Big debate on. I'm leading for the opposition as usual. Fry yourself an egg.'

She had the feeling that she could dominate the scene from the ground. That if she stood next to the headman and talked to them, they would see that no insult to their *mores* was intended, that it had been purely accidental and that their mere self interest dictated that they should accept the I.G.O. deputation.

It was so very obvious to her and the sense of personal invulnerability was so strong that she was out of the car and moving across the white sand before Dag realised what she was about. Spencer was quicker off the mark. Whatever her motive, and it seemed like plain foolishness to him, it was all gain as far as he was concerned. He fairly jumped out of the car's line of fire and was beside her at a run with Vanora's elegant laser pushed against the side of her hat where a hole could only make a basic personality change.

He said, 'Well done, Ginger. Your daddy isn't going to like this at all.'

Momentarily it was stalemate on the European front. Dag could go ahead and liquidate Vanora as a *quid pro quo* for Tamar; but the balance was more apparent than real. Spencer did not greatly care what happened to Vanora, whereas Dag cared greatly what happened to Tamar.

She realised in a flash that she had placed him in an untenable position and looked round, as though seeing the situation for the first time. Closer now to the Cappodanians, she could see that they were changed by the communal anger which had been sparked off. It had a force of its own, that existed and could be felt now that she was in the middle of it. Psychokinesis, the power of mind to work on matter at a distance. Like the power of the crystal in its special way of bodying forth its images in concrete form.

The dilemma was resolved from an unexpected quarter. The crystal itself, for countless centuries a disinterested mind, having relegated its supported functions to automatic, self-regulating systems, had begun to appreciate that the movements of the creatures in its neighbourhood were representing a growing threat to its continuance. Firmly accepting that the first duty of every living thing is to maintain itself in that interesting state, it had consciously accelerated the rate of intake of alluvial sludge to the upper lake, seeing in this an immediate and practical way of sluicing out whatever structure was being built on its banks.

It had listened without much attention to Vanora's broadcast, only speculating that one so perfect in form might well be content merely to be and need not act. The action involved, in bringing down more of these creatures to play out their independent and curious roles on this happy stage, was not regarded as significantly dangerous, until it picked up the reactions of the others. Then it began to see them as a threat to itself. It had listened to enough Cappodanian conversation to have a well-digested break down of the human psyche in its computer depths and it now saw the danger of being regarded as an open cast platinum mine.

When the whirlpool swirl began its first ponderous movement, there was utter disbelief on the round, brown faces of the residents. Time out of mind, there had been one daily performance at the same precise point of the planet's spin. This was the first time there had been a second showing and they looked at it in real awe. Coupled with the discovery of the sabotaged vault it was a lot for one day and the headman was in distinguished company in falling for the reasonable fallacy of *post hoc ergo propter hoc*.

He spoke into a tense silence, which carried his quiet words like a sentence in a crowded courtroom.

'The crystal is angry because the dead have been shamed.'

It had a good press. It was neat and short, carried the stamp of conviction and expressed the mood of the meeting. The rivalry between the two groups of newcomers and the alignment with Vanora as agent of O.G.A. was hardly relevant to the situation. Moved by a common will and feeling themselves to be the instruments of a force greater than themselves, the small men began to shuffle forward across the sand towards the stationary car.

Vanora recognised that it was a complex situation, but could not see that there was anything in it but advantage for her party. If the Cappodanians destroyed Fletcher or he them it was all one. When the Scotian ship came down there would be that much less to bother about. This showed Fletcher up in a bad light. Had she been at the controls of the car, she would have been already moving out.

Speculation was cut short by the sweeping in of the lake to cover the sand up to the wall to the depth of a metre with fast moving water. It ripped into the open door of the car and shoved it bodily up to Marsh's parabola, where it wedged at an angle which put the lasers out of use. It carried Vanora on its surface like a silver leaf. Spencer locked his one good arm round Tamar Kelly's neck, believing that she was too good a hostage to lose down the plug hole and they were carried in a kicking muddle towards the wall. The Cappodanians had regulated their lives from infancy by the tidal flux and managed better automatically. They succeeded in keeping their feet and such was the force of the last pronouncement, even went on with a pincer movement towards the car.

The last image on Tamar's retina, which she carried vividly with her into the choking tide was that the car had begun to lift. It was a bitter truth, but Dag had written her off. He was moving out. A command decision which would have pleased Vanora had she seen it.

It was the most agonising choice he had made in his life. He had a sudden insight into the quirky quixotic working of her mind and saw her action as a kind of total innocence which deserved to succeed. Longer experience of bucking intractable realities made him sure that it would fail, and he was as much sorry on that account—that she should be disillusioned—as on any other. But he could not set aside the habit of half a lifetime. Only the greatest good of the greatest number could weigh with him as a commander. She was an executive herself and must know that he had to do it. The personal issue had slowed him down, his computer did not come up with the inevitable answer on time. He was beaten by the intervention of the crystal.

By the time he had hauled himself back to the console from the rubble heap in the rumble, Cappodanians were covering the car like ants on an abandoned sugar apple. Even then, he would have taken off, but there was no joy. Intake valves were either submerged or silted up. Before he could blow them clear, he was borne down by sheer weight of numbers.

Back on *Interstellar X*, Bruce Charlton was facing difficulties of decision as searching as those of his commander.

The four day time limit was coming up to its expiry point and the communication blanket had effectively sealed off the missing parties as if they had stepped off the edge of a flat earth. He was on his own with it. And also with a revived memory of an error which had jeopardised another mission. Jeopardised was the kind word. When he forced himself to see it whole, he knew that the deaths at that time could only be set at his door.

That time too, it had been a matter of making a decision. He had been forced to choose a course of action on a time lapse. He had made the choice and the men with him had died. There was always the debating point that he had very nearly died himself. Only a fluke had pulled him out of it. A keen communications man, doing a last scan, working against the clock with blown-up pictures, had spotted his prone grey figure in the black dust. The ship had picked him up with only minutes to spare before the mathematical exigencies of that set-up put the asteroid completely out of court.

If that had been all, it would not have been such a bad memory to live with. But he was an honest man and he had to go on and dig out the real root of the fatal choice. He had not gone by the book. Personalities were involved. If Erica Brault had not been there, he would have made the right decision. But at that time, he could not have given the order to move out, believing that it would leave her on the asteroid. So he had kept his section where they were, waiting for her to show up, missing his own scheduled pick up.

In the event, he was doubly wrong. She had been taken off already in a changed plan which could not be communicated to him. His commander had banked on him carrying out his instructions and had read him wrong. Of course, he could not know, either, the special personal link-up. To be fair, it had not been all that plain to anyone else. And ironically it did him no good at all with Erica. She was a dedicated type and had regarded the affair as either inefficiency or a dangerous weakness. There had been no eyelash fluttering welcome with 'You did it all for me, Bruce.' She said, 'I signed the articles, Bruce, and I *can* read. I don't expect and don't want any different treatment from anyone else. I feel responsible for the accident and I don't like it.'

She was right and it cost him a minor death of the heart. It was a kind of verification of the old 'loved I not honour more' bit; and it was an uncomfortable thing to live with.

Now that the time was coming up, he had to decide to leave the majority of the crew on Thirza. Vanora's party could be written off without much thought. In any case it was not an asteroid with a death sentence involved. They could sweat it out for months until a relief ship arrived. But he was concerned about leaving the firm's chief executive and the I.G.O. consul without any attempt to establish that they were still alive. He tried to be sure that he did not follow the book this time just because his independent action had turned out so badly last time. He might have been encouraged if he had known that Fletcher had similar introspective duels with himself; but in his case, when it came to the bit, he was ruthlessly tough minded.

Jacqueline Ann Roth spotted the frigate in its parking orbit overhead and gave him the good news by waking him out of an uneasy sleep.

She said, in her precise, rather metallic voice, excellently suited for tannoy and communications gear, 'A new star has joined the galaxy and seems to be stationary over your cradle.'

Charlton had to suppress a feeling of relief. It could only be that the frigate had caught up and with that overhead, he would have to stay where he was. Any move into an orbit would be mere suicide. He said, 'Thank you. Get it on the screen and blow it up. I'll be along.'

When he arrived in the control cabin, she was doing a fair job with the specialist gear. She had pin-pointed the object and when he took over to do some refined tuning it was already clear that it was a ship.

'Get Les for me.'

He could wait. It was enough to know that a ship was there. Rooney with his uncanny flair would make a better job of bringing the image up. Five minutes later they were looking at a long piratical, military ship. Dark radial lines from the cone and wasp marking on the narrow centre section gave it an unfamiliar look.

Rooney said, 'There she is, all the evil length of her. I've never seen anything like it in the I.G.O. manual.'

'You won't.' Bruce Charlton was shocked out of his own special problem. 'It's an O.G.A. unit. Scotia. They won't wait to ask our intentions. They're destroyers. Mercenary hatchet men.'

'Where does that put us?'

Charlton turned his thumbs down, 'With a full complement, this obsolescent heap might have a one in a hundred chance to manoeuvre clear. As it is I don't see it. What surprises me is that they haven't taken the initiative. Why don't they send in a homing bomb down our rabbit hole?'

'It would be an act of war.'

'That would not weigh with them. There must be some other reason and the most obvious is that in spite of the coincidence they have not seen us. But they'll be doing a grid scan, so it could happen any time.'

'What do we do then?'

'We wait.'

This time he was waiting to complete a scheduled time scheme and it was as bad as exceeding one. Should he take the initiative and move off before time without Fletcher?

Rooney was on duty with him when Vanora's broadcast came at full strength. In some ways it was an affirmation of all the old saws about patience being a good thing. He saw at once, however, that it raised another issue. The Scotian, if he followed Vanora's instruction, would have to move into a shifting orbit until he was placed for a drop on target. That meant they could choose their time and slip away unobserved.

Unless there were other O.G.A. units over the horizon, it was a reprieve, a gift of life to the five of them and he would be following instructions to the letter.

He left Rooney to alert Freya Burleigh and work out the time it would take the Scotian to act on his orders. Roughly, he assessed it himself as two hours before the ship would be able to get down on the given reference. Then he went along to his cabin to think it out. Freya found him there five minutes later. As the only other navigator, she had appreciated the inherent difficulties of the situation more than anyone else. She said, 'Bruce, I've been working it out on that rendezvous of Vanora's. We could make it on a simple trajectory like a missile. It would only take a fraction of the time that they'll take to get there. We could be in and out before they arrive.'

Her plummy voice would have been more appropriate on a vicarage lawn, knocking the neighbour's azaleas. But she was sincere enough.

His face made her stop. He said, 'That I know, Freya, and you know the brief I have. Play back the log if you want to hear it, Fletcher recorded it there. There are no degrees of freedom whatsoever; it is a precise instruction to leave on a time limit and I will not alter it.'

Physically, they were two of a kind and she could tell almost exactly how his mind worked. She knew that there was something more to it and said with great shrewdness, 'Every case has to be taken on its merits, Bruce. It doesn't matter what anybody else would do or what the consequence might be for us. As far as I'm concerned any decision you take is the right one. I know we're an inexperienced lot; but, if you say so, we'll have a go at it.'

He had been sitting at a small desk against the outer bulkhead, slewed round to talk to her, as she stood just inside the door. She was almost as tall as he was when he joined her there, and trapped her with an arm on each side of her head. Light brown hair, thick and short, blue eyes, mild gentle face; she would look much the same for the next thirty years. Incongruous really for space crew. A large, country girl with an aura of floral prints and strawberry teas. 'Thanks, Freya. I'll let you know what I decide. But there isn't anything to decide, the answer's in the book.'

Her eyes were completely accepting, with a kind of total trust. He knew that it was true what she said. Whichever way he decided to go, it was all right and there would be no recriminations. She pushed away from the wall. Momentarily, there was a warm pneumatic pressure against him, then she ducked under his arm and was away out of the door.

In spite of what he had said to her and to himself, he still had to decide.

There was less than a half hour to his deadline. He wondered if she had remembered Vanora's remaining bomb. That could be sited on the navigation console. This latter thought focused his mind fairly on Freya. He was older now though not necessarily wiser. One thing was for sure, it was not a repeat on the Erica theme.

It was some time before the Cappodanians, with their expertise as beachcombers, had sorted out the foreshore into something like order. The car was hauled over the wall by main force and drained itself like a stranded sea shell.

Spencer and Tamar Kelly were pulled out of the debris at the foot of the wall. A timely move for the girl, who was being used as a convenient pontoon for him to keep his head above water. He had wisely decided that the hostage element was secondary to the vital task of keeping him in the political arena as a living force. She was back in a uniform silver grey sheath with her hair plastered in a skull cap. Face deathly pale.

The busy scavengers had dumped her on the pavement. Spencer pulled her to a sitting position, by using a handful of hair as a tow rope, then put his knee in her back and pumped out some pints of lake water. Now that he was all right, he could see the point about having her alive and relatively well.

Lightly floating on the surface, Vanora came ashore hardly wet. She was in time to join a new convocation in session on the strip between the wall and the entrance arch. The water had done nothing to damp off the emotional xenophobia and she could not flatter herself that she was welcomed in as directrice of the tribunal. But she was not put in the dock either and could reflect that all was still well and would be more than well when the Scotian ship came down. Floating had stimulated thought and she was now convinced that Spencer had a point. She would play it along his way and bide her time until they reached a place where her rank meant something; then Spencer would smart.

With this settled, she could take tranquil pleasure in the scene. Fletcher, Cormac, Campbell and Tamar Kelly were against the wall beside the arch. Literally against it. Held there by forked sticks pushed across their throats. It was hard on Cormac, whose throat was on the thick side for the gauge of stick in use and harder on Tamar who was still finding it difficult to stand and put a certain hanging strain on it. If it had been larger or her head smaller, her protesting body would have settled down in a shapely heap.

Dag Fletcher was badly placed to be any real help. He could not get away from the wall. The support he managed to give at extreme reach of his right arm was only marginal but probably kept her from complete suffocation.

The headman was still going on. Justice on Thirza was a drumhead affair. In the small, close-knit community, extreme sanctions were seldom invoked. This time there was unanimous demand for the supreme penalty and the headman had a moment's inspiration in putting an ingenious and popular form to the sentence.

He said, 'The crystal has spoken. The crystal will be executioner. They will be placed on the central pillar and given to the lake.'

It was well received. There was no immediate query about the practical difficulty of getting them there. In fact he had thought of that too. 'Our new allies will be able to take them out to the pillar in their machine.'

Vanora translated that bit for her party and Spencer immediately detailed Marsh and Voller to show willing. Very practically, she added, 'Take them one at a time and make it quick; we don't know how long this off-beat disturbance will last.'

Dag Fletcher had not followed the scenario in great detail. With his interpreter virtually out of action, he could only go on tones. He knew it was not good. The headman sounded as though someone had secretly cut down his kali tree. When Vanora spoke to her *aides* he pieced it together. There was not much time for the bitter reflection that his small delay had not helped Tamar and had put them all in baulk. He was taken first. Ankles strapped by Voller and wrists heaved together behind his back. Marsh had the car mobile again and shot out over the vortex to the central pillar, which was standing clear above a narrow platform of crystal. Voller, and a Cappodanian, hauled him out and propped him against the column. Then the tumbril shot back for the next in line.

Foothold was slippery, as on a half tide rock. The metre-wide shoulder had a slight slope and he had constantly to strain backwards to keep himself from falling into the seething, milky centre of the lake. Through the thin fabric on his shoulders, he could feel the flat, damp surface of the crystal itself. It had a living warmth and communicated a tiny, fast vibration, which itself tended to shuffle him off his perch.

Tamar was next out and she was so patently unable to stand without support, that Voller passed a loop round the pillar to hold her back. Then Cormac and Campbell were slotted in. They took a cardinal compass point each. Looking out like decorative figures on a plinth. Each wearing a round metal hat so that they should miss none of the nuances of the situation.

There was not much to see. Tamar, slowly coming back to full participation in the present, saw that the beach was lined with silent people. If past experience was anything to go by, the lake would not be long before it settled back. It would make supper late; but this was clearly unusual enough to merit some adjustments to routine. Even the women had come out and stood in a bulbous group in front of the archway, an oblong of yellow ochre.

Cormac faced back to where the trolley had been left. Campbell looked out to the eastern rim. Fletcher facing west, saw the gathering of the short twilight and, moving across his piece of green sky, the firefly spark of the frigate getting itself lined up for its run in.

Tamar had an additional burden of guilt. She said, 'Dag?' and had to croak out the word through a gravelly throat.

'Here, present.'

'Just to say, truly I'm sorry.'

'Don't give it a thought. Remember the old maxim on the Adjustment-to-Living tape. Life is one thing *after* another.'

'This has a terminal look about it though.'

'So we move to that other maxim—Set up a plan of consistent goals. That's easy enough. There's just one. Getting off this Inchcape Rock. Can you move at all?'

'Just a little bit.'

'Edge over this way.'

At the extreme point of movement, with the waist rope biting hard, their heads were almost touching. He saw that her golden brown eyes were steady and without fear. It was, however, clear that no amount of contortion was going to bring any knots near any teeth.

She said, 'Does it take long?'

'No, not long.'

'But all your life flashes past.'

'For you, a thing of beauty. It has to be sometime. If not now another time. If not another time, then now.'

A diversion, just out of his line of vision, checked this

stream of philosophical chat. Blazing retro rockets brought colour into the green light and restored her hair to something like its usual flamboyance. He could not see the ship; but he recognised that there was a negative value in being where they were. It could have been worse, particularly for Tamar, if the Scotians had arrived ten minutes earlier.

CHAPTER TEN

A DISCREPANCY in some of the sense clues in his restricting environment was bothering Dag Fletcher. Part of his mind was playing with an irrelevant parody. 'Cormac the Venusian a fortnight dead, Forgot the cry of gulls and the deep sea swells And the profit and loss.' He was trying to bring in the crystal and its metal sifting chore, but was not getting far, because the original was likely to be topical enough. Consequently Cormac himself had to speak twice before he got an attentive audience.

'Commander.' This time it was a shout and Dag said, 'What is it?'

'By pressing my helmet closely to the crystal surface, I have been able to effect a *rapprochement* with the thought processes going on inside. It is a kind of direct transfer. The mind uses mathematical concepts. Its thought is most interesting.'

That was fine, as a piece of pure research. For a moment, its more practical implications escaped Dag and it was left to the five-element syllogist to keep the flag of intellectual curiosity flying. Tamar said, 'Oh, that's nice.' It was a big effort. She was feeling that it would be no bad thing when the plug went in and the water made a kindly period.

Dag had been given time to digest the bulletin from the psychological lab and at the same time sorted out the other matter which had been bothering him just below conscious level. He realised that the ship which had come down could not possibly be the one which had crossed his line of vision.

There was just not time for it to have got into position. Whether that was good or bad was another matter, but it straightened the record and he gave his mind to the Venusian.

'Does this work both ways?'

'Yes, I believe I can communicate. It has long observed these Cappodanians and has a framework of reference for human type ideas.'

'Does it like you?'

'There is no affective tone.'

'A pity. Perhaps you could persuade it to use its force to keep the water from us. Make a little well of power here. Try it, there isn't much time.'

Cormac saw the need for haste and went back to work without reply. Tamar Kelly had edged back to the centre of her side, where the rope had more slack and the agony was marginally less. She said, 'Alternatively we could just say in unison "Go back waves", like the man did to the tide.'

Campbell indulged her by saying 'And what happened to him, then?'

'He was drowned.'

They were silent. A change in the noise of the water announced the end of the vortex. It was slackening and beginning to fill up. Beyond the light of the hydrogen flares, the night sky was now black. Tamar found she was crying. She was glad that she was alone. It was a private thing; though she was crying, silently, from a generalised sense of waste and lost opportunity. For herself, in the sense that here was a very skilled and complicated piece of human engineering being broken by random chance. Almost guiltily she found she was not thinking about Dag at all.

Dag Fletcher, with the rim of his hat pressed back against the crystal was trying to tune himself in. But for him, the result was to make a partial cancellation of the screening effect of the hat. Whether or not it was wishful thinking was debatable, but he believed he could detect something of the two way exchange with Cormac. The Venusian's brain currents were substantially different from those of Earth human types. Whatever was going on was incomprehensible to Dag; but he sensed the urgency of Cormac's contribution.

Water was lipping the pedestal and moving up its slight incline. He edged towards Tamar to carry what comfort there was. But she was out of reach and he did not call her. If she had not automatically sought him out, it was better to leave it at that. Straining to look for her round the pale green edge, he saw the silhouette of the ship that had come in bulked vast against the hillside. Its commander had dropped it neatly into the courtyard. That would tear the place up. Something familiar about the lines drew him to make an agonising twist to see better. Then it was clear. It was *Interstellar X*.

For a second, he felt an upsurge of hope. Then the water was racing round his feet. It was no good. They could not be in time. Then he was angry. Charlton had broken faith and all he would have to show for it would be the destruction of the ship. The frigate must be moving now into the last phase for a landing course. Its commander would have the corvette stone cold as he came in.

Water was rising now like a filling well. It reached his knees and the pace quickened for the final smoothing out of the tundish. It was silent now, 'too full for sound or foam'. He put his head back against the crystal and he was looking at the great mozaic pavement of the under-ground city of Plantos Three. She was there in vivid colour. Smiling through the countless centuries. Even in the mental twilight, the urgency of his real life situation was breaking through. He was asking her if she had a knife.

As *Interstellar X* settled on its hydraulic rams in the courtyard Charlton said, 'Well done all,' and meant it. Every demand of an exacting schedule had been filled out with split second timing by his small, scratch crew.

When he had decided to move in, it was obviously the people's choice and they had backed him with enthusiasm.

Now he was in, he had to act and that was going to be harder. Voller, working like an extension of his computers, reported that he had sighted Vanora and Spencer. Obvious first move then was to ask them what was oclock.

There was no time to finesse. Charlton put out the coolant gas and was ready to leave ten minutes after *Interstellar X* had stopped vibrating. First he had a word on the external speakers to establish intent. His voice was almost unrecognisable, its cold, precise message carried no suggestion that there was room for debate. From the control room he could see Spencer and Vanora standing with a group of small brown men. Attention seemed to be divided between the ship and some phenomenon in the centre of the lake.

He said, 'Spencer, come forward towards the ship. Don't try to go anywhere else. The main armament is trained on the beach.'

Spencer's hesitation was obvious on the scanner. Charlton had put the gunnery control on to his own console, he devastated a long swathe on a ten metre front running out from the ship, through the encircling building. Eliminating a dozen or more Cappodanians who were out of sight. Nothing remained. A clear open road, the raw material of a motorway. He said again, 'Next time, your way, Spencer.'

Vanora was very helpful. 'Go on, Vernon, see what the man wants. Pwomise anything. The Scotians will settle him.' In some ways, the situation was good. All the opposition would be eliminated at once. If she could stay alive for the next half hour she was well ahead of the game.

Spencer had a fair idea of what was going on in her head; but he was already moving forward. She would have to be very careful or she would not see the Scotian ship arrive. He was beginning to think he would be better without her. A long gurgle from the lake and a corporate sigh from the watchers told him that the ritual drownings were accomplished. So that was all right. He could tell Charlton that they had been powerless to stop it.

Charlton left Voller at the console and took Tancred with him. He said to Freya, 'There isn't much time. You have just about a crew. You will take command. Watch. If anything happens to us, get out. Don't hesitate to devastate all this area of the ship is threatened. Spend any time there is in preparing the ship for a crash take-off. Clear?'

Then they were going down the ramp wearing helmets which Tancred had developed from space gear to screen against the pervasive mind field.

Spencer met them outside the arch, blackened and seared from the fire ball of the landing ship. Cappodanians crowded behind him.

Charlton said, 'Where are they?'

'You're just too late, Charlton. Our good commander and his lady were very tactless and upset the natives. They've just disappeared into the bosom of the lake like Excaliber. There was nothing we could do.'

'Where's the car?'

'Right here.'

'Go over to it. You'll be joining them in the lake if we don't find them.'

The crowd parted silently to let them through. The power demonstration from the corvette had made them silent. Coming on top of everything else, it seemed to point the way to a shaky future.

At the car, Charlton waved Spencer and Tancred into the back. 'Keep a laser against his side, Tancred. Use it if he coughs.'

Charlton swung the car out over the lake in the pallid glare of the hydrogen flares.

'Show me.'

'There was a pillar in the centre. Exposed. Temporarily. They were fastened to it. The four of them. When the water covered it, they would be drowned.'

Charlton made no reply and they ran out over gin-clear water which showed the crystal's descending steps in pale green detail. It was not until they were twenty metres from the centre that they could see what had happened.

The shallow hollow in the centre left a fragment of the pillar exposed like a stub axle. Three heads were still above water; Tamar's strained back in torture with the water coursing over her chin.

Fletcher said, 'Cormac persuaded it to make a ring of force here. But there isn't a lot of time. It might suspend its operations any minute.'

Charlton was already swinging below the hovering car and had harness straps from the winch hook under Tamar's shoulders before he cut the rope. Then he gathered in Fletcher and Campbell and the laden car began to edge away.

Dag said, 'Where's Cormac?'

'Sorry, Dag. His head was well below. He's been dead some time. We haven't room for a body.'

Tamar said quietly, 'Himself he could not save.'

Then they were back on the beach with a new mood of anger in the watching Cappodanians as they saw that the lake had played them false.

Dag said, 'Drop Spencer. Call Voller to open the car port. Run the car back to its berth in the ship. We have to get out, at the double.' When Spencer was standing outside, he went on, 'You'll find some soul mates amongst the Scotians. Let me know sometime, how well you consider anarchy works.'

Then they were circling the high tower of the ship to gain height until Charlton could reach the opening bay. As the car slid home and tripped the relay which closed the shell behind it, Dag grabbed the extension of the intercom. 'Commander to control. Action. Action.' Before they were well out of their seats the alarm bleeps were sounding through the ship. In three minutes flat, the entire ship's company was assembled in action stations. Tamar had even found twenty seconds to stand under a hot shower and was grit free for the first time in what seemed like ever.

As the bleeps ended and the count down clicks began, Dag

was doing a racing round-up of the consoles. Freya Burleigh had worked like a veteran in the brief time she had. Trimming jacks had been checked. A course was roughed out on the chart table. Dag saw that it would take them out, but whether it would be good enough as a tactical manœuvre was another matter. With only Jacqueline Ann Roth at the Power console it was going to be very tricky if he had to fight the ship.

Tamar had run a lightning check of the data on the chart table. She came in with her coolest, professional voice. 'Communications to Commander, confirm all data so far presented.' It was worth knowing that it was rock solid, and if they got out of this it would be a log credit to the cadet operators. He also recognised that this was the first direct chat he had had with Tamar for some time. They had virtually gone out of communication. But there was no time now to negotiate terms. He said, 'Thank you, Tamar,' with that much concession to personalities in the spiky jungle of official procedure.

With the sweep hand coming into the last quadrant and the robot mechanisms locked to go, he remembered, belatedly, to ask about Vanora's last bomb.

'Commander to Co-Pilot,' it was fairly snapped out, 'did you find the last anti-personnel mine?'

Charlton accepted the promotion without comment and replied with a similar turn of speed.

'No. Nor did it detonate on recent short trip.'

'Thank you.'

Dag had enough to do now to trim the slowly moving ship as she began to lift out of the courtyard, enveloping the buildings in an intense orange fireball. G began to build. He had time to think that Vanora's last memento must be triggered to a gravity setting. Charlton had not penetrated beyond the gravisphere of Thirza. It would be a different matter when they made height and were accelerating away into deep space. Some one of them would be at the receiving end. At that stage the ship might well survive it. Any one console could be shorted out and worked from command. What about that?

Command was the likely target for the last one. It could still
be run on a decentralised basis. Tamar would set it up. Suppose Tamar had it? He said, 'Commander. Hear this all. Whenever possible continue to check your console for potential
sabotage. You are looking for a button. There may be no time
to disarm it. Get it through a disposal chute. At this stage,
it will fall back on Thirza.'

Then he was watching through direct vision as a distant
line of fire showed the Scotian frigate dropping down to the
pad they had just left. It was a bad day for a clean building
campaign. Though it was likely that only complete rebuilding
would do much for the lakeside complex.

The Scotian had reached a point of no return in his landing trajectory and even as this fact impinged on Dag's mind,
he knew what he had to do. It was unlikely that he would
ever have a better chance and it balanced out his shortage of
trained crew. With some racing calculation he could change
course and pass over the frigate   she settled down. He began
to reel off his demands and Tamar Kelly felt the rising excitement as she pushed herself to the limit to come up with the
answers he wanted.

Interstellar X began to wheel. In atmospheric flight, she
was behaving like a ballistic missile with a special set of
handling characteristics. Dag had not manoeuvred in this way
since his days as Commander of *Petrel*. He could feel the
tension of his crew, they were there with every detail he
wanted, in the split seconds of time which made them simple
summation units of his computer mind. It became a certainty
that they would do it. And the certainty was a shared
thing.

The Scotian commander must have followed them on his
own scanner. As their intention became apparent, he was
obviously trying to alter the frigate's course. But it was too
late. Even as he was feeding in extra thrust, it only became
an over-correction for landing speed. He had to go down
now and take off again. His ship was temporarily incandescent

and the main armament would not bear. *Interstellar* X crossed the site as the Scotian sank briefly on its hydraulic rams.

Dag Fletcher took it as though there was all the time in the world. He had the glowing ship plumb centre on his grid. He squeezed the firing bar with sensitive accuracy and saw the frigate crumble away like a steeple in the path of a cyclone. An asterisk of intense light blotted the site of the lakeside village and the water of the crater boiled briefly to the rim of its surrounding walls. Nothing could live there. Dag had a stab of conscience for the lost life, Vanora's perfection, even the crystal which could never be investigated now, then he was calling new instructions for Jacqueline Ann Roth and she was filling every power need as it came up on an assignment that a veteran power executive might meet once in a career.

Tamar found a lull in the demands on her computers which had kept her in absolute concentration since she had strapped down. Half left, she could see Dag in direct vision. Still, but relaxed, with that deceptively casual slouch against his harness, which she had come to recognise as a sign of total absorption in his part. The side arm of his acceleration couch had black button pushes to turn it through every conceivable angle. Up, down, left, right, rotate. What was the sixth then? It was odd anyway that she should even think about it, she must have looked at that side panel hundreds of times without giving it a thought.

By a sudden clarification she knew why she was bothering. There was no sixth control. Vanora had hidden this one in the open, like the technique for hide the thimble; so obvious that everybody would miss it. It was the same size and shape as the other five buttons and the spacing was exact. So it melded in to the pattern. A neat bit of camouflage. This one would not damage any equipment, it would simply kill the commander.

Almost before that was fully formulated, she was stabbing at the release clips of her straps. G was still high as *Inter-*

stellar X accelerated away from the green planet, but she had also seen the gravimeter. There were only seconds left before the gravisphere of Thirza had thinned out to a frail, tenuous force which would fail to hold the spring tension of the bomb.

Dag's head came round as he saw the movement and she could see understanding in his eyes as she fairly tore the end button of the line from its adhesive anchorage. There was no time, in her estimation, to use a disposal chute, she gripped it against her chest and fell forward over it in the least cluttered part of the floor. Then once again she was doing a personal count down in a terminal situation and hoping that whatever it did it would be quick and would not leave her only partially alive.

She thought she might say, 'It would be inhuman not to be grateful. You're going to have a fair harem in that subconscious of yours.' But it was better to say nothing. Besides, what she was doing had to be done, *because she had thought of it*. It would save Dag, that was good; it would save the ship, that was all right; but mainly it was her own gesture against the inhumanity of space and time. There would never be a better moment to die. There would never be a better time to say, 'I, Tamar Kelly, in full possession of my five wits, a masterpiece of evolution, at this point, *choose* to end my separate identity in this way.'

She could see a number of possible futures, laid out, in instantaneous clarity, like spokes of a wheel whose rim was oblivion. She repeated his line from the lake, 'If it is not now, it will be another time, if it is not another time, it will be now.'

It seemed in fact to be taking longer than she had expected. Hands grabbed her shoulders and Dag himself was there, turning her on her back and forcing open her gauntlet. For a moment, she hung on, as though it was a monstrous invasion of privacy to save her life; but he had torn it free and was at the chute.

Neither of them had reached their couches when the ship

side-stepped as though it had hit an air pocket and Charlton, in the Co-pilot slot, was fighting to stabilise a dual bank of crazily spinning dials.

As he plugged himself in again to the command console, he got the tail end of something from Freya, who was stretched to her intellectual limit as Navigation Executive. He said, 'Commander. Repeat One,' and got it all again, with a lantern slide like a briefing lecture. It confirmed the expectation that the O.G.A. frigate was not alone, the rest of the squadron was coming up. It was a small but adequate task force. In echelon, like a pendant on a jeweller's velvet pad, an armed freighter-cruiser in the centre, no doubt carrying a full technical and diplomatic staff to set up a consulate on the planet. Flanking the queen bee, two more frigates and then, well back, two corvettes. It was a mixed force with one of the corvettes recognisably Scotian from its wasp marking.

Dag Fletcher's first thought was that it was hard luck on his young crew. They deserved better. After their efforts to get *Interstellar X* away, they were definitely due for a homecoming with some honour and an avuncular pat on the head from chairman Spencer. He would have had them all docketted on his personal files to see that they were accelerated up the promotionary ladder. Then for Tamar it was very unsatisfactory. He should have let her make her own way out in her life-enhancing gesture.

He had put the direct scan on to his own screen and was doing a racing estimate of vectors and speeds when the two corvettes began to peel away from the formation. So, this was it, then. He suspended the official drill and said on the general net, 'Tamar can you raise I.G.O.?'

'The signal's strengthening all the time. Yes.'

'Quickly then. Give them the score. Confirm mineral deposit on Thirza and say that an O.G.A. squadron is on the way in. List the present crew with executive ranks as temporarily held. End with the signal for general engagement. We can't escape, so we're going in to attack.'

'Check.'

'Rooney, break out the I.G.O. pennant.'

'Check.'

'Commander to crew. This is going in the log, and on open transmission. Thank you for your loyalty. You have done well, in the best traditions of this service. Steady now, and give me every ounce of concentration you have left. Watch for G. I'm setting a spiral collision course for the cruiser. Take these figures, Freya.'

Interstellar X began to turn. Its new course would take some working out. By the time it was realised what she was doing, it might well be too late for the cruiser to act. Bright wavy lines on the scanner projecting from the nearer corvette ploughed up the space they had lately occupied. The course change had only just been in time. Dag had taken navigation on manual and was his own computer. Trying to assess what he was about would give some electronic brain a frustration syndrome.

Tamar broke into his concentration with, 'Dag, I've had an acknowledgement.'

He was making tiny adjustments to the trim. A sense of triumph was beginning to build in his mind. The cruiser would not escape, even if it was only the molecular trash of *Interstellar X* which hit.

Tamar came on again. 'Dag, I'm getting it loud and clear. There's an I.G.O. task force coming up. They picked up the general attack signal. You are ordered to get clear.'

It was more easily ordered than obeyed. Dag could imagine that the cruiser had him centred on its fire table. She would be waiting for the right range, so that disintegration would be as complete as possible. If he began to veer now, she would fire anyway. What he did not expect to see was that the cruiser would make a frantic effort to break the deadlock itself.

As *Interstellar X* made her last crash change of course for the mission, the squadron ahead dropped out of the scanner

picture in a dive which must have pinned back all personnel
to the depths of their foam cradles. Then he saw why. Creep-
ing into the top left hand section of the grid, came the first
units of the I.G.O. force. A long supership flanked by frigates. Chairman Spencer had done them proud. He must have
pulled out all the stops. It was the Outer Zone Fleet.

The message coming through brooked no argument. 'Attention *Interstellar* X. Admiral Frazer's compliments to Commander Fletcher. You are requested to take the following
course. . . .'

*   *   *

'One thing I must tell you, Dag.'

'Only one?'

They were in the high Space Terminal Grill swaying on its
slender stalk, looking out over the long pale dunes of the
Fingalnan landscape. Tamar blazed with colour amongst the
pale skinned silvery people. She was wearing the green and
gold ceremonial tabard of the European Space Corporation
Service, still proud of the Assistant Controller rank flashes
which had been gazetted by signal on their arrival.

It was almost the end of a month's local leave. Extra per-
sonnel were coming out on the next service flight to take
Interstellar X on the last leg of its return journey with a full
crew. Freya Burleigh, Jacqueline Ann Roth and Les Rooney
were confirmed in full crew status and Charlton was promoted
Co-Pilot. That was satisfactory enough from the service angle.
The political mission to Thirza had been completed by the
Outer Zone Fleet.

When Frazer set down his ships round the crater, there
was no-one to challenge the validity of I.G.O. annexation.
Nor was there any remaining trace of a mental interference
pattern. A certain amount of radio activity on the site of the
remains of the Scotian ship had to be neutralised and when
this had been done, a consulate was established with sufficient
ground force to maintain it.

A curious product of the last activities of the crystal was a small statue of pure platinum which now stood on a jagged podium in the centre of the crater lake. It was Vanora, as she had appeared in the multi-figure representations on the beach. Her exact, classical proportions had made a deep impression on the mathematical mind. In a last concentration of psycho-kinetic energy, it had transmuted all free platinum in its growth system into a reproduction of her perfect form. It was virtually priceless. Later it was to become the symbol of the planet, engraved on coinage and embossed on the official seals. An ironical twist which would have pleased Spencer had he been anything but atomic dust.

There had been a silence, which was so companionable that he did not want to break it. She was sitting chin in hand with her face averted and her personal acoustic cowl of springy red gold falling forward against her wrists.

Now she turned directly to face him, eyes candid and warm, demanding truth. 'Well, one in particular just now. It's a confession really. You know in the ship when I saw that button. I didn't want to get it. The first thing that came into my head was a kind of relief that I'd located it and it wasn't on my console. Then I knew I had to do something about it, because I was the only one who could. I couldn't have lived with myself afterwards if I'd let it go. Whether it had been you or not, I mean. That's what I'm trying to tell you. You don't owe me personally a thing for that. I wouldn't want you to carry a burden of gratitude round like an old man of the sea. Do you mind?'

Compromise in human relations is an excellent technique. He said, 'I won't mind if you won't mind.'

'What do you mean by that?'

'I cut you out on the beach. I was moving off when the water brought us down.'

'That's not the same. You had to do that.'

'It's near enough the same. In a way it's a good thing. We know both that in the last analysis you have to do what you have to do, and only yourself can decide that. Fortunately, these crises are well spread out. In the interim, there is a good deal of living in the world as it is. And for that it is best to identify with a group.'

'What group did you have in mind?'

'A very select group of two in the first instance. One being a distinguished and gorgeous red-head.'

He stood up, towering over the small silver-haired steward, who hurried forward to make courteous, chair-moving gestures, and held out his hand. Very brown in white drill. Green-grey eyes meeting the brown ones in a look that was without haste or anxiety, but expected the answer—yes. As the elevator took them down in a gravity drop, he said, 'Enjoy your last hours of freedom, young Kelly, before the group door closes on you with a definitive click.'

She said, 'I'll lock the door myself and keep the key where you won't get it without a very intimate fight.'

Conscious of the maxim that one should treat sex with the same attention as any other main problem, he gave this the full benefit of his computer mind and came up with the conclusion that it was pillow talk. When the elevator sighed to a stop and its ribbed-tray floor moved them gently out into the crowded foyer, they were unaware for some minutes that it was so.